"I want to make it clear that I will pay for my dinner and Ellie's."

Evan shook his head. "I invited you."

"No, you didn't," Julia said. "Your daughter did."

"That's the same thing." His sharp gaze drilled into her, his mouth firmed in a hard line.

"Sorry, I pay my own way."

He smiled. "Did anyone ever tell you that you're stubborn?"

"Oh, on a number of occasions."

Evan glanced toward the doorway that led to the hall. "While the girls are still playing, I have a question. Why did you correct me earlier when I called you *Mrs.* Saunders?"

* * *

Homecoming Heroes: Saving children and finding love deep in the heart of Texas

Books by Margaret Daley

Love Inspired	Love Inspired Suspense
The Power of Love	*Hearts on the Line*
Family for Keeps	*Heart of the Amazon*
Sadie's Hero	*So Dark the Night*
The Courage to Dream	*Vanished*
What the Heart Knows	*Buried Secrets*
A Family for Tory	*Don't Look Back*
*Gold in the Fire	*Forsaken Canyon*
*A Mother for Cindy	
*Light in the Storm	
The Cinderella Plan	
*When Dreams Come True	
*Tidings of Joy	
**Once Upon a Family	
**Heart of the Family	
**Family Ever After	
A Texas Thanksgiving	

*The Ladies of Sweetwater Lake
**Fostered by Love

MARGARET DALEY

feels she has been blessed. She has been married more than thirty years to her husband, Mike, whom she met in college. He is a terrific support and her best friend. They have one son, Shaun. Margaret has been writing for many years and loves to tell a story. When she was a little girl, she would play with her dolls and make up stories about their lives. Now she writes these stories down. She especially enjoys weaving stories about families and how faith in God can sustain a person when things get tough. When she isn't writing, she is fortunate to be a teacher for students with special needs. Margaret has taught for over twenty years and loves working with her students. She has also been a Special Olympics coach and participated in many sports with her students.

A Texas Thanksgiving
Margaret Daley

Steeple
Hill®

Published by Steeple Hill Books™

Special thanks and acknowledgment to
Margaret Daley for her contribution to the
Homecoming Heroes miniseries.

STEEPLE HILL BOOKS

Steeple
Hill®

ISBN-13: 978-0-373-81382-7
ISBN-10:   0-373-81382-1

A TEXAS THANKSGIVING

Enter into his gates with thanksgiving and into his courts with praise; be thankful unto him and bless his name.

—*Psalms* 100:4

To three special girls,
Ashley, Alexa and Abbey

Chapter One

"Am I glad you are finally here, Julia. I need help!"

Olga Terenkov, dressed in a jean skirt with a leather vest, cowboy boots and large pieces of turquoise jewelry, planted herself in front of Julia Saunders.

"What's the problem?" Julia asked and placed her cherry pie on the dessert table.

"Too many pets. When I decided to have Show and Pet for the children, I never thought they would bring everything from a boa to a pig! Those are not pets!" In her exasperation, Olga's Russian accent became heavier.

"And my daughter just brought a goldfish," Julia said and peered around the grief counselor to search for Ellie among the crowd of parishioners at the church picnic. Her daughter had raced toward her friends the second she'd climbed from the car. Ellie stood in the middle of a group of children showing them her new and only pet swimming in its plastic bowl.

Leading a pony, a little girl with light brown shoulder-length hair joined the group of kids. Her daughter immediately latched on to the cute animal, holding her small fishbowl in one hand and stroking the pony with the other. Ellie, even though she was only five, wanted to learn to ride ever since they had arrived at Prairie Springs from Chicago four months ago. Julia was sure she would hear about her daughter's renewed longing later that night.

Olga gestured toward the newest arrival. "See? Next someone will bring a rat."

"What can I do to help?"

"I need someone to get the Show and Pet organized, to be in charge. I thought all we would have were a few cats and dogs. Where are the normal pets?" The older woman threw her arms up in the air. "I've got Paige's dad to help, too. I need all the animals moved over there." Olga pointed toward an area roped off with a few temporary pens set up. "Can you do that for me?"

"I was supposed to help Anna with the food."

"Oh, she's got more than enough with David, Caitlyn and Steve. See?" Olga fluttered her hand toward the end of the long tables.

"Then, sure. I'd be happy to help with the pets." This from a woman who had never owned a pet, except now—a low-maintenance goldfish. Julia spied her friend Anna giving instructions to a small army of volunteers and wished she could take back her words. She would be better handling the food.

"Who's Paige's dad?" Julia asked, still learning all the children's names. This was only her third Sunday attending Prairie Springs Christian Church.

"You see that handsome cowboy over there?" Olga nodded her head in the direction of the group of children Ellie was in the midst of. "That's Paige's dad, Evan Paterson."

Julia found the man Olga indicated. He was the picture of a quintessential Texan cowboy one would see in an ad campaign. His image had plagued her dreams since her first glimpse of him from across the room at Ellie's elementary school. Her daughter had talked about Paige, but Julia hadn't realized the connection between Ellie's classmate and the tall, lean man with sandy brown hair and the bluest eyes she'd ever seen.

"I'm surprised you don't know him. Paige and Ellie are in the same kindergarten class. That's Paige with your daughter. She brought the pony."

For a few seconds Julia studied the little girl, who had befriended her daughter, before she again found herself zeroing in on the Texan cowboy. "I saw him at Back to School Night a few weeks ago, but we didn't meet. I didn't realize he went to this church."

"He goes to the early service, and don't you attend the late one?"

"Yes."

"Well, then I will introduce you two, and you can start getting that menagerie under control." Olga spun around and moved toward the group of children.

Julia heaved a sigh and followed. Every alarm in her body went off the closer she came to the kids and Evan Paterson. There was something about the man that reminded her of—

"Evan, I want you to meet Julia Saunders. I've talked her into helping you with the animals."

He pivoted toward them, tipping back his black cowboy hat, his mouth cocked in a grin. "Pleased to meet you, ma'am."

"Likewise." Julia fit her hand in his and shook it. His firm, self-assured grip left a warmth on her palm that she couldn't quite ignore.

"I'll leave you two to work this out—" Olga swept her arm across the scene in front of them "—before we have animals running loose all over the place. Now I wish I had gotten more pens."

At that moment one of the Mayhew twins let go of her large dog's leash while turning her attention to the pony. The black Lab darted through the group of children and made a beeline for the food table. Quick, as if he was used to roping dogs, Evan leaped forward and snatched up the end of the leash. The Lab came to a grinding halt a few feet away from the desserts.

Olga clapped. "Very good. For a second I thought we were at a rodeo."

Julia chuckled at the "aw, shucks" look that appeared in Evan's eyes and the touch of color that brushed lightly across his cheeks.

He lowered the brim of his hat to shield his expression and gave the leash back to the little girl. "Josie, keep a tight rein on your dog."

Before Julia could say anything, Evan put his two fingers in his mouth and trilled an ear-piercing whistle that silenced the clamor. "I need everyone to get their pets and move over there." He pointed toward the corded-off area.

Olga leaned close and whispered to Julia, "That's his military training. A cowboy in uniform. You can't go wrong there."

Then Olga hurried away, leaving Julia speechless for a good minute. She'd heard from Anna about her mother's "little matchmaking" schemes, and now Julia was sure she had become the object of one. Little did Olga know that she wasn't in the market for anything that looked remotely like romance.

When Julia swung her attention back to the problem at hand, she realized she was standing by herself while all the pets and children headed toward the area Evan had indicated. He was more organized than she was.

"That man doesn't need any help," she muttered to herself and started forward.

Julia came up behind Evan. "Reporting for duty." She curled her hand to keep from saluting.

After directing his daughter and her pony to one of the pens, he wheeled around, pushing his cowboy hat up on his forehead to reveal the amusement in his eyes. "It's hard to get away from something that was a part of my life for years. When faced with overwhelming odds, I always fall back into my military training."

"And come out fighting?"

His laughter peppered the air, the crinkles at the corners of his eyes that gave him character deepened. "I was a sergeant and used to giving orders to the men in my unit."

"Then if you've got everything under control, I'll go help Anna with the food."

"And disappoint Olga?"

"Then you know what she's up to."

"I've known Olga for quite some time. She can be a steamroller, a sweet one but nevertheless a determined one, too. I find it easier to go along until she is out of view."

Uncomfortable with the topic of their matchmaking, Julia searched for a safer subject to discuss. "So, you've been a member of this church for a while?"

"Yes, and you're new. How long have you been attending? This is the first time I've seen you here."

"Three weeks. I tried out some other churches in Prairie Springs, but this one fits my spiritual needs."

"Help! I've lost my kitten!" a little boy shouted.

The twenty-pound "kitten" jumped over a

rabbit's cage and landed on the pig's back, sending it charging forward. The cat continued its trek through the animals, causing a mutt and a German shepherd to chase after it while dragging their owners. After scurrying up a nearby oak, the pet that started the chaos perched itself on a top limb, staring at the dogs barking at the bottom of the tree. A picture of the cat in *Alice in Wonderland* popped into Julia's mind.

Shaking the image from her thoughts, Julia hurried into the melee. She intended to calm the children who still had control of their pets while Evan waded through the dogs by the oak tree. He grabbed the collar first of the mutt, then the German shepherd and hauled them both to their waiting owners.

Cradling the fishbowl in her lap, Ellie sat next to Paige. Both girls giggled.

Julia stopped in front of her daughter. "I'm glad someone thinks this is funny."

Ellie put her hand over her mouth in an attempt to contain her laughter. "Taylor did that on purpose. He wanted to see what would happen, Mommy. He thought the dog was funny earlier."

Julia knelt by her daughter and Paige. "Can

I count on you two to help me?" After both
girls nodded, she continued. "Paige, put your
pony into the first pen while I get the pig into
the second one."

"What about my goldfish?" Ellie still held
her bowl.

"I don't think we have to worry about your
fish getting away. You can set it up on something high enough where the other animals
won't bother it," Julia said, smoothing Ellie's
brown wavy hair back from her face. "Honey,
if you and Paige can get all the kids with dogs
over there—" Julia pointed toward a roped-off
area at the far end "—that would be a big help."

"When is Show and Pet gonna start?" Paige
tugged on her pony's reins.

"When we have some kind of control on the
situation." Julia prayed those weren't her
famous last words concerning this activity.

Two hours later Evan stood off to the side
watching Julia supervise the kids while they
showed off their animals and let anyone who
wanted to pet them. She would make a great
sergeant in the army. Not only efficient and
hard-nosed when she needed to be, but she'd
also organized the children and their pets while

he'd climbed the ladder and brought down the "kitten" that had started the whole mess.

By the time he was back on the ground, he didn't have anything to do except observe her in action, a petite woman with long wavy brown hair and eyes the color of a new leaf on a maple tree. Every movement had a purpose, but when a child needed extra attention she was there to give it, even to the little boy who had caused the commotion with his cat.

Leaning back against a pole, where a goldfish bowl resided, he folded his arms across his chest and let his daughter give some of the smaller children rides on her pony, Sugar. Paige had wanted more responsibility and this was as good a time as any to give her some.

Julia Saunders approached him, a smile deep in those green eyes. He lowered his gaze to her full-lipped mouth, set in a smile directed at him. For a few seconds a trapped sensation took hold of him until he shook some sense into himself. No way was he going down that path. Ever. Again.

"Your daughter's pony has been a huge success. This is Ellie's second ride." She stopped next to him and immediately the scent of lavender wafted to him.

"She wanted to bring all her pets. I put my

foot down and told her only one. Now I'm glad I did. That's all we need is more animals."

She arched an eyebrow. "Oh, you don't think forty-four is enough?"

"You counted them?"

"In order to keep up with them."

A woman after his own heart. He was liking her more and more. And that was the problem. He didn't need a woman in his life.

Evan pushed off the post. "I'd better get Sugar back in the trailer. We need to be leaving."

"So soon?"

He swung his attention to Julia. "I thought the picnic was winding down. I've seen a few families taking their stuff to their cars."

Two patches of red colored her cheeks. "I meant—I…" She averted her gaze. "My daughter is going to be disappointed that Paige is leaving. They have been inseparable today."

"I've noticed. She's mentioned Ellie to me a few times. I didn't realize she was your daughter."

The picture of Julia, dressed in a pair of black slacks and a red jacket with black trim, materialized in his mind. The first time he'd seen her across the kindergarten room she had been talking with the teacher, her hands gesturing as she spoke. He could almost tell what she was saying by their movements. Very expressive.

He'd made his rounds looking at the pictures the students had drawn of their families and home, then at some of his daughter's work on her desk. Although the whole time his gaze kept straying to the petite woman with Sarah Alpert, he stayed across the room. He knew trouble when he saw it.

"Ellie's birthday is in a few weeks. I haven't been here that long. Where's a good place to have a birthday party?"

"All I've heard from Paige is about how great The Amazing Pizza is. According to my daughter, it has everything a person having a birthday could want. Rides, games, food, all indoors under one roof. She's already working on me for hers in January."

"Thanks. I'll look into it." She slid him a look. "Unless you think Paige would be upset if Ellie had hers there before she did?"

Evan chuckled. "Hardly. If I told her I was taking her there every weekend, I would have a happy camper." He saw his daughter and Ellie heading for them. "But don't say anything to her about it. I want to surprise her. She thinks we're gonna have it at the ranch."

"She doesn't want it at the ranch?"

"No way."

"Ellie would love to have her party some-where like that. All she talks about is learning to ride a horse."

"Sometimes we don't appreciate what we have," he said in a low voice.

"Daddy, can Ellie come spend the night tonight? I want to show her my other pets you wouldn't let me bring."

"I have some work I need to do when I get home. I don't…" He swallowed his next words when a disappointed expression descended over his daughter's face. He was being manipulated, but Paige had been through a rough nine months. Her mother had died suddenly of a drug overdose, and now her aunt, Evan's little sister Whitney, was missing in action. "Sure. That is, if Mrs. Saunders says yes."

"Mommy, can I?"

Julia's gaze flitted from one girl to the other, then settled on him. "Are you sure? We can make it another time if you have work to do."

"No, that's okay. The girls can help me."

"Then it's fine by me."

Paige threw her arms around him. "Thanks. We'd better get moving then." She whirled around and raced toward Sugar tied to a post with Ellie quickly catching up with her.

"That quick exit is my daughter's way of saying let's get out of here before he changes his mind," he said with a chuckle. "I'll bring the girls to church tomorrow for Sunday-school class."

"That's great. I'll pick her up here then."

The girls approached with the pony. Ellie grabbed her fishbowl off the post and hugged it against her chest.

"Do you mind following me to my apartment so I can pack an overnight bag for Ellie? I don't think that outfit will look too good for church tomorrow." Julia gestured toward her daughter, whose jeans and long sleeve striped shirt were dirty. "It shouldn't be too far out of your way."

"Mommy, why don't you bring it out later before you go over to Anna's tonight? We have a lot to do before it gets dark."

"I could," Julia replied with hesitation in her voice. "I haven't been on a ranch yet. We didn't have too many in Chicago."

"Daddy has a big one. It's the best in Texas." Paige tugged on the reins and led Sugar toward the horse trailer.

As the girls walked away, their heads bent

together, Evan sighed. "I think we're being manipulated."

"You think?"

Evan strode toward his truck with Julia beside him. "The ranch isn't too far outside of town. It's on Johnson Road about three miles out. I have a sign over the entrance that says the Double P Ranch."

"Double P?"

"After Paige. It's all for her. Her heritage."

Julia retrieved the fishbowl from Ellie before she climbed up into the cab of the pickup. "I'll be there by six."

Evan opened the back of the horse trailer and took the reins from his daughter. "We'll still be at the barn. Stop by there, Mrs. Saunders."

After Paige scurried to the passenger door of the truck, Julia said, "It isn't Mrs. Saunders but Miss Saunders. I've never been married," then strolled toward her dark green Ford Mustang.

Julia drove east on Johnson Road, tapping her fingers against the steering wheel in time with an eighties tune blaring from the radio. She was running a little late and hated to be since she was usually on time unless Ellie was involved.

She'd had her hand on the doorknob heading

out of her apartment when the phone rang. She'd thought about ignoring it, but as a social worker, she knew emergencies occurred even on a Saturday night.

"Mommy, I need ya to bring my movie, *The Parent Trap*."

Ellie gave her directions where to find her treasure box with the DVD in it. Julia smiled at the thought of the items in her daughter's decorated shoe box. There was a plastic horse that her daughter had informed her was exactly the kind she wanted for her birthday, a picture of the two of them together in front of the apartment building in Chicago and a stack of letters from Grandma….

Thinking of her mother brought back memories that ladened her heart with sadness. Ellie hadn't seen her grandmother much, even though they had lived in the same town for most of her young life.

Tears misted Julia's eyes. *I'm sorry, Dad, Mom. I'm so sorry.*

She swiped at her cheeks and focused ahead on the asphalt pavement.

Suddenly, a loud pop exploded in the air, and her Mustang jerked to the left toward the ditch alongside the highway. She swallowed the panic down and tried to gain control of her car. She turned the steering wheel to the right but it was too late.

Chapter Two

I've never been married. In his barn Evan stabbed the pitchfork into the hay to fill his wheelbarrow. She'd said that then left him to wonder what she'd meant, especially by the almost defensive tone in her voice. A warning? It shouldn't mean a thing to him, but it did. He would chalk it up to his curiosity, except that it was more than that.

Julia Saunders intrigued him.

Against his better judgment.

If she'd said it to warn him away, then she didn't need to worry because the last thing he wanted to do was get involved with a woman. Not after Diane.

If she'd said it to shock him, she clearly didn't know him well. He didn't shock easily, not after his experiences in the war. He'd seen the scope of human tragedy.

And human joy.

Life and death, at its elemental core.

"Daddy, we cleaned out the stall. Can we ride the horse now?" Paige skidded to a stop in front of him with Ellie right behind her.

"Let me finish putting fresh hay in the last one, then I'll saddle Bessie for y'all to ride."

"We're really gonna get to ride a horse?" Ellie asked his daughter as they strolled to the mare's stall.

Evan stared at the darkening sky beyond the opened barn doors, then checked his watch. Ellie's mother was late. Thirty minutes, which for some reason surprised him. He figured her to be someone who would be on time. He shrugged and loaded his pitchfork with more hay. He'd been wrong before about a person— disastrously so.

The strains of "The Battle Hymn of the Republic" blasted from his jean pocket. He laid the tool against the wheelbarrow and retrieved his cell phone.

"Paterson here."

"Evan, this is Julia." Her voice was quivering.

His military training taking over, he straightened, checking to see where the girls were. After he found them, he continued to sweep the area. "What's wrong?"

"I'm in a ditch along Johnson Road, I'm guessing not too far from your ranch."

"Are you hurt?"

"No—at least I don't think so. Just shook up."

"What happened?" His grip on the phone strengthened about the bit of plastic while his gaze fastened onto the two girls at the other end of the barn—safely out of earshot.

"I had a blowout. My tire is shredded. I lost control and went into the ditch." Exasperation leaked into her voice. "I don't have roadside assistance. Do you know a good wrecker service?"

"Yes, I have a friend who works on cars and has a gas station. I'll call him and get him out there, then come pick you up."

"You don't—"

"What are you going to do? Walk here after he takes your car away? We'll be out to get you in a few minutes. Bye."

He cut the call off and then punched in Carl's number. When his ex-army buddy came on the line, Evan told him about the situation and that he would meet him out on Johnson Road.

Three minutes later Evan started his truck

with both girls sitting in the front with him. Dark shadows crept across the flat terrain.

Ellie squirmed around to peer up into his face. "Are you sure Mommy is okay?"

He gave her a grin and what he hoped was a reassuring look. "That's what she told me. We'll pick her up and bring her back here, then you can check for yourself."

"My mommy is the bravest person I know. She banged her head last month and didn't cry at all."

"My daddy doesn't cry. He fell off a new horse last week and got right back up on him."

"My mommy…"

Trying desperately to contain his laughter, Evan turned onto the highway and tuned out the two dueling girls. There was no way he would get into the middle of that.

Almost a mile from the ranch's entrance, Evan spied Julia and her Mustang off his side of the road in a three-foot ditch, which meant she'd gone across the lane of oncoming traffic when she'd lost control. She could have been in a bad wreck if anyone else had been on the road. The thought churned his stomach.

Ellie pointed. "There's Mommy. She's waving at us."

"I don't see the front of the car." Paige sat forward as much as her seat belt would allow.

He parked as far off the road as he could near the back end of the Mustang. "You two stay in here."

"But, Daddy—"

"Paige, no argument. It's getting dark and it's not safe being out on the highway." The second he'd said that he'd realized his mistake.

"Mommy's not safe?" Ellie asked, her eyes showing worry.

"Yes, she is, but I know how little girls can get. I'm switching on my blinkers." He didn't want the two of them worrying anymore. "That will alert anyone that there's a stalled car on the side of the road."

As he climbed from the cab, Paige said, "Be careful, Daddy."

Ever since his wife had walked out on his marriage on Thanksgiving Day two years ago, Paige got scared easily, even a couple of times to the point where she'd become hysterical. He'd left the army earlier than he'd intended to raise his daughter, but her fears only escalated after Diane died of a drug overdose.

Evan strode to Julia, first assessing her, then the Mustang. Even in the dim light of dusk, he could tell that the tires were on their last thousand miles, if that. He motioned toward the nearest one. "Were you going to drive until there was no rubber left?"

She pulled herself up tall. "I beg your pardon."

"Those aren't even good for a tire swing."

"I was going to get a new set in November right before winter weather sets in."

He tipped back his hat, feeling the waves of indignation coming off her. "We don't have that much winter weather—not like Chicago. November starts next week. You need to have Carl change all of them or you'll have another blowout."

Her chin lifted. "Just as soon as I get the money to pay for them."

If he wasn't mistaken, a northern chill had just blasted past him. "And while we're at it, I would suggest getting a road-assistance service. There can be some pretty lonely stretches of highway outside of town. And since you are single—"

"I also plan on doing that," Julia cut in, "when I can swing the money, but so you won't worry about me, I don't plan on driving outside of town."

"You did tonight." Evan removed his hat and slapped it against his leg.

"Point taken." She swung around toward the sound of a vehicle approaching. "Oh, good, the tow truck."

"After he hooks up the car, I'll take you back to the ranch."

"He can't fix the tire after he pulls my Mustang from the ditch? I have a spare in the trunk."

Evan chuckled and set his hat back on his head. "Ma'am, there's a possibility there are more things wrong than just a flat tire."

"What do you mean?"

"Carl will need to get it up on a rack and check the underside of your pretty little Mustang. I know because I once drove into a ditch and had three thousand dollars' worth of damage, mostly not visible."

"Oh."

Her crestfallen expression tugged at him. From what she'd said about having to save money for the tires, he was ninety-nine percent sure she didn't have a lot of cash sitting around for big emergencies. "You do have car insurance?"

"Of course." Offense marked her voice and her face now. "But I have a thousand-dollar deductible."

Carl limped toward them, wearing his usual

Dallas Cowboys' cap, jeans and T-shirt. "Whatcha got here, Paterson?"

"At the best a ruined tire." Evan waved his hand toward the car. "At the worst major under-carriage damage."

Carl studied the Mustang for a long moment, removing his ball cap and scratching his head. "I'll take her down to the station and have a look. I'll give you a call in an hour or so and let you know."

"I appreciate it. We'll be at the ranch." Evan indicated she go first toward his pickup.

"But—" Julia started to protest, took a look at him and shut her mouth.

As Julia slid into the passenger's seat in front, the two girls scrambled to the back and sat. On the short ride to the ranch, all Julia heard was Paige and Ellie whispering. She couldn't figure out what the children were saying, but she got the feeling it was about Evan and her. No doubt they sensed the tension between them.

Yes, she was grateful that he'd come and picked her up, but he didn't have to be so high-handed. He fit right in with the military personnel she had worked with while in Prairie Springs, taking command, inflexible in his attitude, with an air of authority.

Please, Lord, let my Mustang only need one new tire. I don't have a thousand dollars for the deductible if the damage is extensive.

Evan parked by the barn. "I have one more stall to finish, then we can go up to the house. Do you mind?"

The man stared straight at her with a penetrating look that for a few seconds robbed Julia of any coherent thoughts.

One of his eyebrows shot up. "Do you, *Miss* Saunders?"

She would have to explain, and the reason she had told him in the first place—practically a stranger—was to discourage any further interest in her. She'd never done anything like that, surprised at her statement to him almost as much as he had been, because she guarded her privacy, especially her lack of marital status.

"No, of course not. I've missed dinner with Anna as it is. I called her and told her I couldn't come after I called you earlier."

Paige leaned forward. "Good, then you can stay and eat with us after Ellie and I ride. Daddy, you didn't forget you promised us we could after you finished your chores?"

His mouth tilted into a grin. "If I had, I

wouldn't admit it now. But we aren't eating here at the house, Paige. I don't have anything. Grandma comes tomorrow with our meals."

"Comes with your meals?" Julia asked before she realized she was sticking her nose into his business, and she definitely didn't want to give the impression he interested her. Which he didn't.

"I am the first person to admit that I'm a lousy cook. Paige's grandmother prepares our dinners and a couple of lunches and delivers them to us twice a week." His grin notched up another degree. "I can manage breakfast. It's not too difficult to pour milk over cereal or pop a frozen waffle into the toaster. So I'm not totally inept in the kitchen."

"I probably wouldn't let Carmella's know about your skills. I don't know how you could handle being a chef and a rancher."

His eyes narrowed. "I think you're making fun of me."

"There is no thinking about it. You are a single father. You should know how. I would be glad to give you a few lessons, that is if you are up for it." The second the words were out of her mouth, Julia wanted to snatch them back. Why in the world had she dared him? He was the type of man who couldn't resist a challenge. She wanted to spend less time with him, not more.

"You've got yourself a pupil." He shoved open his door. "When do you want to start?"

"Tonight?" Could she teach him everything he needed to know in one short lesson?

"Not gonna happen unless we want to eat at midnight. I don't have any food in the house to cook, unless you can whip something up with a box of cereal, some milk, chips, soda and ketchup."

"I'm good, but even I can only do so much."

"Then we go out for dinner and delay our lesson till some other time."

Over the hood of the truck Julia asked, "How about tomorrow afternoon? Tell you what. I'll bring some groceries over then and give you a lesson."

Paige and Ellie shouted their enthusiasm for that plan.

"Daddy, that means Ellie can have another riding lesson tomorrow."

Ellie gave Paige a high five. "Yeah! Two in one weekend!"

The two girls wheeled around and raced for the last stall. Bessie poked her head out, and Ellie stroked her.

Evan removed his wallet from his back pocket and took some money from it. "Here, use this to buy the groceries."

Julia observed the huge smile on her daughter's face and shook her head, realizing where all this had been going. "If you'll teach Ellie to ride, I'll teach you to cook. Fair?"

Evan stuffed his money back into his wallet. "You've got yourself a deal." A chuckle slipped past his lips. "But I think I got the best part of this deal."

She didn't. She hadn't seen her daughter so happy since they had moved from Chicago. Coming to a new town hadn't been easy for either of them, but she had been determined to start over, fresh, without the past hanging over her head. Chicago held too many memories for her. In the past five years, her mother had seen Ellie three times. Her father had never seen his only granddaughter, and yet they had lived just ten miles from them. That had been difficult to explain to her daughter, that Julia's father had disowned her and Ellie because of Julia's mistake.

Standing at his back door leading into the kitchen, Evan shouted at the retreating figures racing toward Paige's bedroom, "I want you two to wash your hands before we leave for dinner."

His daughter abruptly stopped in the entrance to the hallway and put her hand on her waist. "You have to, too, Daddy." She waited until he made his way to the sink before whirling around and continuing on to the back of the house.

"I suppose I'd better, or Ellie will nail me when she comes back in here." Julia stepped up next to Evan, and found his scent of leather and hay surprisingly pleasant.

"Yep. Nothing slips past them." He finished and placed the dish towel on the counter for Julia.

She ran the warm water over her hands. "I want to make it clear before they return that I'll pay for my dinner and Ellie's."

"I invited you."

"No, you didn't. Your daughter did."

"That's the same thing." His sharp gaze drilled into her, his mouth firm in a hard line.

"Sorry, I pay my own way."

"Did anyone ever tell you that you are stubborn?"

"On a number of occasions."

Evan glanced toward the doorway that led to the hall. "While they're still gone, I have a question. Why did you correct me earlier when I said Mrs. Saunders?"

Thankfully, she'd prepared herself for this question. In the past when people asked her about her name, she didn't go into too much detail other than to say she was single. Most didn't pursue the topic, especially since she didn't encourage them. "I am a single mother and always have been. I didn't want there to be any confusion concerning that."

"I get the feeling you've had to defend your choice to others."

My choice? Being a single mother hadn't been her choice. She wanted to marry Ellie's father—he was the one who had run off, disappearing from her life. Julia lifted her chin. "No, because I won't. It's something that's personal, and if someone has a problem with it, then I'm sorry but it won't change the facts. Ellie is the best thing that ever happened to me."

"I know what you mean. That's the way I feel about Paige. Ah, I hear them coming."

Relieved that was over with, Julia rinsed her hands and dried them as the two girls came into the kitchen. Her gaze strayed to Ellie. Her daughter looked a lot like her father, and he hadn't even cared. A child hadn't been in his master plan, so he'd conveniently vanished right before Ellie was born, leaving her to deal with everything on her own, even the medical bills.

She'd trusted Clayton and lost so much, but at least she'd gained a precious daughter. It had been Ellie's impending birth that had led her to seek the Lord. Jesus had opened a whole new world to her that she shared with her daughter— a world where mistakes were forgiven.

"I'm starved." Paige wiped her wet hands on her jeans.

Ellie followed suit. Julia cringed, remembering the mare her daughter had sat on not that long ago. She started to say something about washing again, then decided Ellie would live.

"We need to hit the road. I'm starving." Evan let the two girls leave first, then indicated for Julia to go after them.

The ringing of his phone halted his progress toward the door. Julia paused in the entrance while he answered it.

"We were just heading out." He listened for a moment, then said, "Thanks, Carl. We'll be by later, after we take the girls to dinner." When Evan hung up, he faced Julia. "The only other damage was a few dents and scrapes. He will replace the tire for you with a similar type unless you want something else."

She shook her head. "No, that's fine." Not knowing much herself about cars, she was sure Carl knew what was best.

"Then let's get these kids fed so you can pick up your car."

And get home. This evening hadn't turned out at all as she had thought it would. At least she didn't have to come up with the deductible. It had taken her five years to pay off her medical bills after having Ellie. She was finally getting on her feet financially.

Thank you, Lord.

Evan stood at the window that afforded him a view of his yard and front pastures that bordered the highway into town. A cloud of dust coming down the road that led to his house announced a visitor. The blue sedan told him it was Marge Freeman, his mother-in-law, with her food delivery.

Lately, she had been hinting at moving in with him and Paige, so she could make fresh meals daily instead of bringing them twice a week. He was grateful for her help, but he didn't want her living with them. Her presence was a constant reminder of his wife's betrayal—one he wished he could forget. But there was no way he would deny his daughter access to her grandmother. She had so little family in her life, especially with his little sister, Whitney, deployed.

Evan turned away from the window and crossed the living room to go into the kitchen. Why wasn't there any news about his sister? She continued to remain lost in a Middle East war zone. Had she been captured? Was she dead? These questions plagued him day and night.

"Grandma's here," Paige said, racing into the kitchen and through the open back door.

Evan followed his daughter outside to help bring the bags of food inside. "Good to see you, Marge."

The large woman struggled out of the car, placing her hand at the small of her back. "I'd have been here sooner if my uncle hadn't taken so long to eat his lunch. That man is the slowest eater in Texas. Molasses flows faster than he eats." She grinned, a flush tinting her cheeks. "Of course, Uncle Bert ends the meal with telling me he has to savor every little bite because it's five hours to the next one. Can't stay mad at someone who says that."

"Grandma, what did ya bring us?" Paige opened the back door and stuck her head into the first sack sitting on the car seat. "Mmm. Chocolate chip cookies. I love those." Evan's daughter started to delve into the bag for a sample.

"Paige Paterson, you know better than that. You can't have any cookies till after you've eaten a good meal."

Marge's rebuke hadn't surprised Evan. She'd said the same thing to him on several occasions. He and his daughter would indulge after she was gone. He'd learned pretty quickly not to argue the point with his mother-in-law, not when he was beholden to her for preparing so many meals for Paige and him. At least he paid her for them, against Marge's protests, but he was Paige's provider.

"Yes, Grandma. I forgot. They just smell so good."

"That's because I just took them out of the oven not thirty minutes ago."

Evan drew in a deep breath and relished one of his favorite smells. "Let's get this inside."

After the food was put away, Marge took a look around the kitchen, then made her usual trip into the living room. She stopped short of pulling out a white glove and running it along the woodwork. After church, Paige had picked up around the house while Evan had run the vacuum cleaner and dusted, but his mother-in-law always found something to silently criticize. It was her way of telling him he needed her in his life full-time. As much as he wanted Marge to spend time with his daughter, he would hire a housekeeper before he would resort to his mother-in-law living with them. She needed to control everything around her. They were too much alike.

Marge bent over, groaning from the effort, and picked up a white string from the medium brown carpet. Moaning some more, she straightened and walked to the trash can in the corner and threw away the offending piece of thread. Then she pointedly looked him in the eye, wordlessly stressing his need for her.

He had to learn how to cook. He couldn't keep going through this twice each week. Paige could visit her grandmother at her house, where he wouldn't get the *look* he'd come to dread.

"Thank you again, Marge, for everything you do for Paige, and me." Evan started back toward the kitchen, hoping the woman would follow. He caught sight of the clock on the wall near the stove. He didn't even want Julia and Marge to pass each other on the road that led to his house.

"I have a picture I drew for you," Paige said from the living room. "I'll go get it."

Tension in his neck streaked down his spine. Maybe he should have explained to his daughter that her grandmother and Julia shouldn't meet, especially when the young, beautiful woman would be bringing a sack of food for his cooking lesson. That definitely wouldn't go over well. She was due any minute. It was possible she would be late again. He could only hope.

Evan moved back into the living room as his daughter came forward with a watercolor picture of a horse—though the only reason he knew that was because Paige had told him.

Marge gushed over the painting as if his daughter was the next Monet. "This will go on my refrigerator just as soon as I get home." She sidled toward the lounge chair as if she were going to settle in for a long visit. "I love your use of colors. When I was a little girl, I always wanted an orange cat."

"Grandma, it's a horse—Bessie."

"Oh? Well, Bessie looks great."

"Speaking of Bessie—" Evan latched on to the mare's name "—have you fed your pony?"

Okay, it was a stretch since the pony was called Sugar, but he was desperate to have Marge leave before Julia showed up. There was absolutely nothing between Julia and him, but he didn't want to try and explain that to his mother-in-law. She had been sure his reluctance to date anyone was because he still loved Diane, so she took every opportunity to rewrite what her daughter had done—walking out on him, turning to drugs. Now that she was dead, he didn't have the heart to straighten her out.

"I did when I got home from church."

"And you've done your other chores in the barn?" Marge hated the barn and wouldn't go near it. Much too dirty for her.

Paige nodded. "I'm all ready for Ellie's lesson."

Oh, great.

Right on cue, Marge's head swung around toward him, and she gave him the *look*. "Ellie? Who's Ellie?"

"My best friend. We go to school together. She's coming out here this afternoon. Daddy is teaching her to ride."

Okay, he might be able to get Marge out of here still without bringing Julia's name into the conversation.

"I didn't know you gave riding lessons. I

have a friend whose granddaughter would love to learn."

"I don't usually." Evan immediately realized his mistake and bit down on the inside of his mouth.

"He's teaching her because Julia's teaching Daddy to cook."

"Julia? Who's Julia?" Her look knifed through him.

"Ah, she's…" He searched for a way to make it sound as if he wasn't betraying Marge or her deceased daughter. "She's…"

"She's Ellie's mom," Paige chimed in. "She spent the night here last night."

"What?" Marge's eyes widened to the size of round platters.

"No. Paige meant Ellie. *Ellie* spent the night here." His face felt on fire from embarrassment and Marge's searing gaze.

Silence descended for a long moment, broken by the sound of footsteps on the front porch and a loud knock at the door. *Caught red-handed.* He would never hear the end of this.

"They're here." Paige clapped and raced to the entrance before Evan could move or think of a way of getting out of the awkward situation.

Chapter Three

The large woman who stood directly behind Paige as the child opened the front door caused Julia to take a step back. Irritation puckered the lady's thin lips into a frown, its full force directed at her.

Evan appeared and moved around his daughter, blocking Julia's view of the unhappy woman. "Come in, y'all." He took the grocery sack she held and hurried toward the kitchen, hiding the sack against his chest.

Julia advanced inside with Ellie next to her. Immediately, Paige dragged Ellie off toward her bedroom, leaving Julia to face the lady who was still frowning at her.

Evan came back into the room, minus the items she had picked up for their cooking lesson. "Marge, this is Julia Saunders. Ellie's mother."

Julia held out her hand to shake, but Marge just looked at her, ignoring the greeting. Julia dropped her arm back to her side and said, "It's nice meeting you."

"Marge is Paige's grandmother."

Evan's mother? But there was no way Julia would ask that question out loud.

The large woman turned toward Evan. "May I have a word with you in private?"

"Sure." Then to Julia he said, "I'll be right back. Make yourself at home." After the last sentence, he cringed and darted a glance at Marge.

As the two left, Julia sagged back against the wall near the front door. She felt as though she had interrupted something. Julia wanted to leave.

Instead—because she knew it would upset her daughter if they left early—Julia made her way back to Paige's room. She didn't want to overhear any comments between Evan and Marge. The two girls sat on a white-canopy bed with a cotton candy–pink coverlet over it.

Julia leaned against the doorjamb. "Are you ready for your second lesson?"

Ellie peered at her. "Yes! I dreamed about

riding last night. I can't remember what happened, but I woke up happy."

The slamming of a door rattled Julia. She stiffened, then tried to relax so the two children didn't think anything was wrong. But they heard the same sound, and both of their foreheads crinkled in question.

Before either of them said anything, Evan came down the hall, arranging his features in a calm expression when he stepped into the girls' view. "Are you two ready to go ride?"

"Yes!" they shouted in unison.

Ellie leaped from the bed and hurried toward the hallway. Paige moved at a slower pace and paused by her father.

"Is Grandma all right? I thought she might stay and see us ride."

"She needed to go home to Uncle Bert, so she couldn't."

"I wish she would watch me ride sometime."

"She will, princess."

Smiling now, Paige rushed after Ellie.

"Obviously, I came at a bad time," Julia said, trailing after the two girls.

Evan asked, "Did they hear Marge leaving?"

"'Fraid so."

He winced. "That's what I thought. My

mother-in-law didn't understand why I wanted to learn to cook. She is perfectly content to fix our meals forever and she made that crystal clear to me."

"So, that wasn't your mother?"

"No! My mother died when I was a child. My father now lives in Dallas."

"Why wouldn't she want you to learn to cook?"

"Because she enjoys preparing our meals, but especially coming out here and showing me just how lacking I am in housekeeping skills. She's angling to be our housekeeper, although she would hate ranch life."

Julia surveyed the kitchen with its clean counters and lack of dirty dishes in the sink. "I'd say you do a good job."

"Not according to my mother-in-law. She believes her granddaughter lives in a pigsty."

Julia stopped next to the oak table with two yellow place mats on it. "You're kidding! I was considering hiring you to come over to my apartment and clean it."

Julia liked the sound of his laughter that suddenly warmed the small space between them. Any lingering tension from Marge dissipated as his gaze captured hers. Her heartbeat picked up speed.

He broke eye contact with her, focusing on the bag on the counter. "What are we cooking today?"

"Spaghetti."

"The kind in a can?"

She shook her head. "I think you've probably mastered that. Let's move on to something more challenging."

"Are you sure that's wise? I once boiled an egg that exploded in the pan because I forgot about it."

"I'm sure. But I like to live dangerously."

"You might regret saying that before this is over." He looked beyond her to the back door. "We'd better get to the barn before my daughter has Bessie saddled and decides to give her own lesson."

"She's good for her age. How long has she been riding?"

"Almost two years. Since I've had the ranch. She was so enthralled with the horses that I was afraid she would try to ride on her own if I didn't teach her." He grabbed his cowboy hat from a peg near the door.

"Paige sounds more and more like my Ellie. No wonder they like each other." Julia left the house first, conscious of Evan's gaze on her as she descended the steps on the back stoop.

"I'm not sure if I'm glad or scared. Paige can be a whirlwind."

Julia slanted her glance toward him as they strolled to the barn. She could easily picture him riding over his land, saving a calf that had fallen into a hole, mending his fences, breaking a wild horse—everything but being a cook.

"Why didn't you just say cook the onions?" Evan crunched up his mouth, his eyebrows beetling, as he stood at the stove brandishing a wooden spoon in his hand as though it were a weapon.

"Because a recipe will say sauté. If you're going to cook, you need to learn the terms, too. Words like whisk, brown, fold, caramelize."

"Why would I caramelize anything? I don't even like caramel."

Julia pressed her lips together to keep from laughing out loud, but a chuckle or two escaped. "When you caramelize something like diced onions, you cook them until they are a caramel color."

He pushed his hand through his hair. "All I want to learn are a few dishes so Paige and I won't starve. Today has confirmed that I can't continue to be so reliant on Marge. Now I discover I have to learn a whole new language. I'm almost afraid to ask what fold means in cooking. I know how to fold laundry."

"First, stir the onions before they burn."

Evan complied, muttering something under his breath that he at least understood the word burn.

"When you fold something in, you slowly add it to a mixture, gently turning over the batter as you do. For example, you might fold strawberries into a cake batter. You wouldn't want to stir them too vigorously."

"No, I'm sure I wouldn't."

"Now that the onions are clear and the meat is brown, it's time to add the rest of the ingredients, turn the heat down and let the sauce simmer."

"Is *simmering* in cooking similar to a temper simmering?" He dumped in a can of diced tomatoes. Some of the liquid splattered on him and the stove.

"Yes, like browning meat is just what it means. You'll want the meat to turn brown—not black or stay pink." She gave him a dish towel to wipe his hands.

"But I like a steak red."

"That's a steak, not ground beef. You don't want it red or pink when making a sauce."

"This isn't gonna be easy, is it?" He added the tomato paste.

"You'll get the hang of it." She hoped, and sent a silent prayer to the Lord for guidance. She loved to cook but had never taught another person how. "My plan is to teach you to prepare a few meals that children like to eat. Things like macaroni and cheese, spaghetti, pizza."

"Pizza? You don't just order it from a restaurant?"

She laughed. "Believe it or not, some people actually make it in their homes."

"I guess stranger things have happened." He put in the last of the spices that she had taught him to measure earlier—or rather, demonstrated how. "Done."

Julia pointed to the knob on the front of the stove. "Turn it down halfway between low and medium. Now we'll get the water on for the spaghetti."

"That shouldn't be too hard. I do know how to boil water."

"Unless you leave an egg in it too long."

"Spaghetti doesn't explode, does it?"

The smile he sent her caused a fluttering in her stomach. "Not to my knowledge, but you can overcook it." She gestured toward a pot, trying to dismiss her reaction to his heart-melting grin. "Let's fill it three-quarters of the way and put some salt in."

He followed her instruction, placing the water on the burner. Julia handed him the salt. When he sprinkled it into the liquid, she turned to put the spices away in the cabinet next to the stove.

When she glanced back at him a minute later, she caught him staring at her, still sprinkling salt into the water. She clamped her hand around his wrist and yanked it back. "What are you doing?"

He looked down at the pan. "Putting salt in the water like you said."

"A little of it goes a long way."

"I didn't use a lot."

Her gaze connected with his. The fragrance of onion, tomatoes, spices and ground beef cooking teased her nostrils. The sound of the water beginning to boil competed with the ticking of the wall clock. But for a few seconds none of that really registered. All of her senses centered on the man being so close. She could smell a hint of lime in his aftershave lotion. The depths of his eyes glinted a smoky blue. She felt the pull of them.

Giggling from the living room dispelled the

moment. When he looked away, she realized she was still holding his arm and immediately released her grasp, backing away a few steps.

"Uh," she grappled for something to say, "why don't you put a little oil into the water?"

"Why would I want to do that?" His face scrunched up in an expression of horror.

"Because the spaghetti will clump together after it's cooked if you don't."

"You see? How in the world will I ever learn all these little tricks?"

"It takes time. You won't learn to cook overnight." Although she wished he would, so her job would be done. She grabbed the bottle of oil and passed it to him. "Just a little." After he finished, she continued and said, "It's time to put the spaghetti into the water and turn the heat down to medium."

Completing the task, he stood back and eyed the pots on the stove. "What's next?"

Julia held up her finger, glanced over her shoulder and said, "Girls, do you want to come on in here, instead of lurking in the doorway, and set the table?"

"How did ya know we were here?" Paige appeared from the right side of the entrance.

"Yeah, Mommy, we were being extra quiet."

Ellie shuffled into view from the left side and positioned herself next to her friend.

"I could have super hearing, but in this case I heard two little girls giggling rather loudly a moment ago."

"Are we gonna be able to eat the food?" Paige entered the room and clasped the back of a chair at the table.

"Do I detect doubt in my daughter? This is gonna be the best spaghetti y'all have ever had. Isn't that right, Julia?" When she didn't say anything right away, a stricken look descended on his face. "You're supposed to stand behind your pupil. After all, isn't that a reflection on your teaching ability?"

She had her doubts since she realized she should have had Evan throw out the water he had salted and just start over.

"Girls, I'm going to let you be the judges. A teacher shouldn't. I don't want to discourage the pupil." Julia removed four dinner plates and glasses from the cabinet and placed them on the table.

While Paige and Ellie set the table, they kept peering back at Evan and Julia at the stove and whispering between them, which immediately caused several giggles to erupt.

Julia leaned close, lowered her voice, but not too low so the girls couldn't hear and said to Evan, "I think my next teaching job is to show Paige and Ellie how to load the dishwasher and clean up. I don't think six is too young to learn that." She winked at him.

"Mommy, I'm five. I won't be six for a couple of weeks."

"Oh, right. You think Evan and I should do the dishes then?"

Ellie nodded, a serious expression on her face. "You'd better. I'm still too young."

Julia couldn't suppress her laughter any longer, its sound sprinkling the air. She spun away from her daughter in time to see the water boiling over. Quickly, she snatched the pot from the stove. A burning smell floated to her as she dumped the pasta into the strainer in the sink.

"A word to the wise, don't let little munchkins distract you from your cooking," Julia said as she switched off the heat on both burners. "Is the table finished?"

"Yep." Paige pointed to the nearest place setting, her shoulders thrust back, her chin held high.

Next to the little girl, Ellie imitated her friend's stance. "We did good."

Other than the six pieces of silverware at each plate, Julia had to agree. "Then let's eat. Bring your plates over to the counter and take the spaghetti you want."

Five minutes later with dinner served, Julia took the last vacant chair next to Evan and sat. "Who would like to say grace?" she asked when she noticed Evan reaching for one of his three forks to eat.

He stopped and looked at her. "Oh, yeah. I will." He bowed his head. "Father, please bless this food and the people at this table. If You can find the time, You might help me learn how to cook. I could sure use Your help. Amen."

When Julia murmured amen more enthusiastically than usual, he shot her a look, similar to the one she had seen Marge give him. She tossed him a grin and a wink.

"What did you think of me riding today?" Ellie shoved her fork into the pile of spaghetti. "I'm doing it by myself. Pretty soon we can all go riding together."

Julia paused in bringing her glass of water to her lips. "Well, honey, there's just one thing wrong with that. I don't know how to ride."

"Mommy! You don't? I thought every grown-up knew how."

"We can take care of that. The next time I give you a lesson, I can give your mother one, too."

Ellie clapped her hands. "That's perfect!"

"No, it isn't. You might like to ride those big animals, but I don't think I want to."

Ellie's eyes grew round. "Why not?"

"I…" Up until June, she'd lived her whole life in Chicago, and hadn't even once been to a farm.

"Yeah, why not? Scared to let me be the teacher?"

Evan's dare taunted her as he knew it would. Julia bristled for a few seconds and said, "Okay, I'll learn, and I'll learn how to ride faster than you'll learn to cook a simple dinner by yourself."

"I'll take you up on that challenge."

"Daddy, when are you gonna give Ellie her next lesson? Next weekend?"

"I can't. I have to set up for the school carnival Friday afternoon and evening and then work it on Saturday."

"So do I." Julia finally took a long drink of her cold water. Instead of staying away from the man, she found herself planning ways to be with him. Probably not a good idea, but she didn't know how to get out of it gracefully and not disappoint her daughter.

"Then we can do it next Sunday after church."

"Fine, and I'll give you your second cooking lesson. We'll make pizza."

"Only if you give me a list of ingredients to buy."

She inclined her head. "That's fair. I will before I leave tonight."

"Pizza! I love it, Daddy." Paige finally took her first bite of the spaghetti and scrunched up her face. She quickly swallowed her food, then took several gulps of her milk.

"What's wrong, princess?"

"Nothing." Evan's daughter stared down at her plate.

He slipped a forkful of his creation between his lips and surprise flashed into his eyes. When he got the spaghetti down, he coughed. "Maybe we can drive into town and get some hamburgers at Prairie Springs Café. My treat."

Since it looked fine, Julia was curious how bad the food tasted and put a small amount into her mouth. A salty taste exploded against her tongue and she washed it down with a long drink of water. "Just how much salt did you put in the water while my back was turned? You said it wasn't a lot."

He shrugged. "I don't know. I didn't think it was. I like salt." Gesturing toward his food, he grinned. "Obviously, it was more than I thought. I must have been distracted."

A blush stained her cheeks. "Now you know why salt goes a long way."

"And then some," he said and rose, taking his and Julia's plate to the sink. "The good news is I don't think the sauce tasted too bad."

Julia crossed to the stove, dipped the wooden spoon into the red mixture and nodded. "Not bad at all. There's hope for you. I'll save this in your refrigerator. There's enough here for another meal. You can pick up some more spaghetti while you're at the grocery store. Just don't put too much salt in the water when you cook the pasta."

"You're gonna trust me to do that without your watchful eye?"

"I'll write the instructions down with your grocery list. I think you can follow simple directions."

"I'll help ya, Daddy."

"You've got yourself a date, princess."

Paige threw her arms around his waist and hugged him.

A lump formed in Julia's throat. She'd wanted that for her daughter—a father who loved her. Instead he'd vanished one day, leaving only a brief note telling her not to bother looking for him, that he wanted nothing to do with being a father or a husband.

Evan pounded the nail into the board. The noise level was already loud, as the elementary school gym was crowded with parents helping to set up for the carnival the next day. But no Julia Saunders. He should know. He would catch himself looking around every few minutes, expecting to see her, then get mad at himself, more determined than ever to focus on building the booth he'd been assigned to by Olga. Then something would catch his attention and before he knew it, his gaze would wander to look for Julia.

Yes, they'd all had a pleasant evening last Sunday, enjoying a nice meal at Prairie Springs Café before going their separate ways. When he'd returned home, he didn't even have anything to clean up. Julia had insisted on doing it before leaving for the café since he insisted on paying for dinner. He'd tried to talk her out of it, but she was one stubborn woman. She'd informed him she paid her own way and did her share of the work, always.

It was as if she was determined not to take

anything from him. Why? Had she been burned like him? That had to be it or she would have been married to Ellie's dad. Curiosity bubbled to the surface, but he immediately squashed it down. Two wounded souls had no business getting together.

"The carnival is tomorrow, not next weekend, Evan." Olga planted herself in front of him, blocking his view of the rest of the gym. "And we only have eighteen hours until the doors open."

"I'll have it finished within the hour."

"Good, because I've decided to add a petting zoo, especially after the success of the Show and Pet at the church picnic, and you can be in charge of it. Isn't that perfect for a rancher?"

No, he thought. "In where? Here? There's no room left to put another activity."

"I listened to the weather today and tomorrow it's supposed to be beautiful, so I thought outside, but you'll need to make some temporary pens for the animals."

Evan rose from kneeling on the floor and stretched. "Where are the animals gonna come from?"

"Where else? Your ranch. You have tons of them." She flitted her hands near his face, her large turquoise bracelet with silver beads tinkling.

"I don't have enough for a petting zoo."

"How can you not? You have a ranch with horses and cattle."

"Which aren't easy for kids to pet. They're too big."

She tapped her finger against her jaw. "Then I will contact a few people I know who have some interesting animals and have them bring them first thing tomorrow morning. Can you get here by nine?"

He nodded, remembering the fiasco of her "Show and Pet" at the church picnic last week and all the incidents that Olga had conveniently forgotten. At least this time he was in charge from the beginning and hopefully could control the situation.

"That's great. I will have an assistant for you. You will not be alone."

As Olga scurried away, he thought the woman was too late. He was very alone. And that wasn't likely to change anytime soon. That was the way he wanted it. Much safer.

He began to turn back to the booth he was constructing when he caught sight of Julia entering the gym. He paused and studied her. Her long brown hair appeared mussed, as though she had been running her hand through it repeatedly. Worry furrowed her forehead and dulled her eyes.

Before he realized it, his legs were chewing up the space between them.

Something was wrong.

Chapter Four

Evan stopped Julia before she had time to step more than a few feet into the gym. "Hi. Is everything all right?"

Her concerned gaze fell on him, and she swallowed hard. "No. I was at the office when I received a call from Dr. Nora Blake, the heart surgeon that performed little Ali's operation. His grandfather, General Marlon Willis, was just admitted to the hospital. He's had a massive heart attack, and it doesn't appear he will make it. Dr. Blake called me because Ali would be without a guardian if he dies. I'm the social worker assigned to his case."

"Ali has gone through so much. I hope the general makes it. He hasn't had a chance to get to know his grandson for long." Evan moved closer. "Is there anything I can do?"

Julia shook her head. "It's wait and see time. I thought after I finished here, I would go to the hospital and check on what's happening. I want to be there for Ali. If his grandfather dies, he's going to feel so alone." Sadness jammed her throat. She knew what it was like to be alone without family for support.

"Doesn't Sarah live next door to the general? I saw her earlier in here. Do you think she knows?"

"Probably not if she's been here. It just happened. From what Nora told me, the general had come to the hospital to see Ali when he had his heart attack. In that sense, he was lucky. He was able to get help quickly."

Evan turned toward the crowd in the gym and searched it. "That little boy has been through so much in his short five years. He's already seen too much death. Ah, Sarah's over there." Evan pointed toward the far corner.

"I'd better have a word with her. Where will you be?"

With a flip of his hand, he gestured toward a half-finished booth under a basketball hoop. "And if I don't get back there and complete my job, Olga will be breathing down my neck. She's already informed me that I need to step it up."

"After I see Sarah, I guess I'd better check in with her and see what she has planned for me."

As if hearing her name, or else realizing Evan had stopped working, Olga approached, asking, "Is your booth finished?" Her gaze leveled at Evan.

"Almost."

"Well, hop to it. That petting zoo won't get set up by itself." While Olga shooed him away, she turned to Julia. "I'll need you to help him with the zoo. You two are a great team."

Team? Olga was definitely working overtime as a matchmaker. "Where is this petting zoo going to be?" Julia asked, scanning the gym for a space big enough to house the animals.

"It'll be outside."

"But it's been raining a lot lately. Do you think that's a good idea?" *And while we're on the topic of good ideas, I don't think Evan and I should team up. That means I'll have to spend practically the whole weekend with him.*

"We cannot have it in here—there's no room." In her usual dramatic way, Olga swept her arms wide to take in the whole gym. "After the way the children responded to the pets at the picnic, we need to have a zoo. It will be a hit."

"Fine," Julia said, seeing no way of getting out of assisting with the petting zoo. She sure hoped Olga found another couple soon to play matchmaker with. "I'll help Evan, but I have to speak with Sarah first."

"But—"

"I won't be long." Julia hurried away, leaving a frustrated Olga by the entrance.

Julia made a beeline for the redheaded teacher, who was putting the finishing touches on a booth. "Sarah."

The slender woman spun around and smiled when she saw Julia. "Did you just get here?"

"Yeah. We need to talk. I got a call from the hospital right before I left work."

"Is it Ali?" Concern darkened Sarah's blue eyes.

"No, he's fine. But his grandfather is in the emergency room. He had a heart attack."

"Oh, no." Sarah pushed the brush toward Julia. "I've got to get over there. Does Ali know?"

Julia gingerly took the brush from Sarah, white paint on its handle as well as the bristles. "I don't know. Probably not, until the doctors know more."

"Can you finish this for me? I promised Marlon I would take care of Ali if anything happened to him."

"You did?"

"Yes. Since he has no other surviving family, he asked me to be Ali's guardian, should anything happen to him. His heart condition has been worsening, but he wanted so much to be there for his grandson."

"Have any papers been signed?"

"No. We hadn't gotten that far."

"I've been assigned to be Ali's social worker. Even if the general does survive, Ali will most likely need a foster parent. You would be perfect."

"That shouldn't be a problem, since I was one last year." Sarah shed a large man's blue shirt that had splashes of milky-white paint everywhere. "As you can see, I'm messy with a brush. I doubt Olga will ever ask me to do this again."

"Remind me not to ask you to help me with my apartment." Julia laid the brush across the lip of the gallon can on the tarp on the floor. "I'll be over there later. I need to pop in and see Ali."

Later, Julia arrived at the emergency room with Evan right beside her. He had insisted on coming to the hospital and had followed her for the entire thirty-minute drive to Austin.

She slid him a glance. "I didn't know you knew Ali's dad, Greg?"

"We were stationed together in the Middle East for part of the time. Greg didn't have much to say about his dad, except that the general had disowned him when he married Ali's mother."

"Disowned?" The word stung her, and she couldn't help thinking about her own relationship with her father—or rather the nonexistent one.

"According to Greg, his father had other plans for him that hadn't included marrying a woman from the Middle East."

"It's hard to understand how a parent could do that. I could never disown Ellie."

"I know what you mean. But sadly, it happens. Some parents have a certain plan for their child, and when it doesn't occur, they get angry."

"Yeah, I've heard that," she murmured, not sure she could ever share with another person the pain and disappointment her father's actions had caused her.

Evan approached the nurses' station. "How is Marlon Willis?"

"Are you family?"

"No, friends. Has he been moved to a room?" Evan asked the receptionist behind the counter.

"Julia!"

She wheeled around. Sarah rushed toward her, her eyes red. A sinking feeling gripped Julia's stomach. "What's happened?"

"Marlon died about half an hour ago. I've just been sitting in the waiting room trying to decide how to tell Ali."

"I'll go with you if you want." Julia's throat closed. She'd only met Marlon a couple of times, but she knew what Ali had gone through recently. Orphaned, the terrified little boy had been flown to America for emergency heart surgery, and was taken in by a grandfather he had only just gotten to know. His prognosis was good and he was expected to live a normal life, at least physically. But what little boy could emotionally withstand losing three parental figures in such a short time span?

"Would you? This isn't something I had anticipated doing anytime soon." Sarah started for the elevator but took a detour toward the women's restroom. "I'll pop in here. I can imagine how I look. I don't want to frighten Ali before I have a chance to tell him."

Evan stood next to Julia while they waited for Sarah. "Ali's had to deal with quite a bit of loss."

"Yeah. Both my parents are alive." *Alive and well but not part of my life.*

"My mother died when I was twelve. I can still remember when my dad told me. I didn't believe him at first. He was never the same after that, and now with Whitney missing in action, I don't know what will happen to him if she is found dead."

"Hopefully, he'll turn to the Lord to help him deal with it." As a social worker she had become very attuned to a person's pain, even when masked. Evan and Ali had a lot in common. Maybe he could help the boy.

Evan looked away. "My dad has lost his faith."

"Maybe you can show him the way back."

Evan kept his gaze glued to the elevator door. "That might be a little hard since I can understand where he's coming from."

Julia placed her hand on his arm. "I thought you believe—"

He stepped away, her hand falling to her side. "I never questioned God until I saw so much death in the Middle East. I kept thinking, what kind of God would allow a man's legs to get blown off? And now, since Whitney is missing, probably dead, I have a hard time keeping my faith. I feel like I've been hit from all sides."

Like Ali. *One crisis after another can do that to a person, Lord. Please help me to show Evan the way back to You. He needs You more than ever, but instead he's turning away.*

"The Lord is your comfort in those times."

The door to the restroom swung open, and Sarah emerged with her face freshly scrubbed. "How do I look?"

"Fine. Are you ready?" Julia glanced from Sarah to Evan, aware of the sudden distance between her and Evan, as though he had regretted sharing that part of himself.

Silence reigned on the elevator ride and short walk to Ali's room. Julia paused at the child's door and let Sarah go first. The thin boy seemed so small in the hospital bed, an IV on one side and some kind of monitor on the other. When he saw Sarah, a huge grin flashed across his face and his large, soulful eyes lit up.

"Sarah, you here," Ali exclaimed with growing confidence in his use of the English language.

"Yes, I couldn't miss visiting you, even one day." Sarah covered the distance between her and Ali and took his hand in hers.

The boy peered beyond Sarah to Julia and Evan, a question entering his gaze.

Julia advanced to Sarah's side. "It's so good to see you again. I wanted to tag along when Sarah told me she was coming to see you." She turned slightly toward Evan. "This is Evan Paterson. He was a friend of your father's."

"He was?" The dimple in Ali's left cheek reappeared as the child swung his attention to Evan. "Howdy."

"Yep. We served together in the army."

"Army! Do you know Dr. Mike?"

A frown briefly chased away Sarah's smile, but she pasted it back on her face. Julia remembered Anna telling her that Sarah and Mike Montgomery were once engaged.

"Yeah, I know Dr. Mike, too. I understand he was a big help to you."

Ali nodded. "Yes."

"Well, I had to meet the guy who has everyone rooting for him."

"Rooting?" A tiny furrow lined the child's forehead.

"Cheering for him. Clapping for him."

When Evan demonstrated, Ali's expression brightened again with understanding. "Like football?"

Evan nodded. "You've got the idea."

"Ali, I need to tell you something," Sarah said after a long pause.

The five-year-old boy looked back at her. "Yes?"

Sarah drew in a deep breath, slid a glance at Julia, then said, "Your grandfather came to the hospital today."

"I haven't seen him." That furrow returned and deepened in the boy's forehead.

"Yes, I know. He didn't have a chance to come up here. He wasn't feeling well, so the doctors examined him. They did everything they could, but he was very sick and he passed away a while ago." Sarah swallowed hard, tears filling her eyes.

Puzzlement dominated the child's expression. "Sick? He passed what?"

Julia wasn't sure he fully understood what had happened. Evan began speaking in a foreign language that the child obviously followed with no problem. At the end Ali murmured yes, his eyes wide, as though he didn't know what to think.

Ali stared at Sarah. "He is gone like Mama and Papa."

Sarah cupped her other hand over their

clasped ones. "Yes, he is, but you're going to come live with me."

Evan again said something to the boy who peered back at Sarah. "Live with you? When?"

"Yes." Sarah broke away long enough to scoot a chair close to the bed. "Your grandfather wanted it that way. When you leave the hospital, you'll go to my home."

Evan translated for Sarah.

Ali blinked. A tear loosened from his eye and ran down his cheek. "Not go home?"

"My home is your home now." Sarah pointed at herself then Ali.

"Home." Ali closed his eyes, his head rolling to the side as exhaustion descended.

Sarah brushed back the child's dark hair from his forehead. "Yes, home," she whispered.

"Sarah. Good." His eyes popped open for a few seconds before sliding shut again.

Sarah looked from Julia to Evan. "I'm going to stay here for a while in case he wakes up and has questions. Evan, I didn't realize you spoke Arabic."

Evan shrugged modestly. "I pick up languages easily, and since I spent quite a bit of time in Ali's country, I learned it. Although he has a pretty good grasp of English, I wanted to make sure he understood what was going on."

"I'm glad you were here." Sarah smiled her thanks.

"Me, too." Julia acknowledged yet another thing that intrigued her about Evan. "Sarah, I'll get everything rolling on naming you Ali's foster mother. That way he can come home from the hospital with you. I don't want his life disrupted any more than can be helped."

"I appreciate that."

Julia moved toward the door and waited in the hall for Evan, who appeared a few minutes later.

"I offered to translate for her if she needed me. I also told her I would work with Ali to teach him more English. He's picking it up, but Sarah wants him to start school as soon as his health allows him."

"That's very kind of you." Julia walked toward the elevator.

On the elevator ride down to the ground floor, Evan stared at the lighted panel before him. Speaking Arabic after all this time brought back memories of the war he had hoped to keep at bay—witnessing a good friend's death not a week after he had arrived for his tour of duty;

a bomb exploding and killing civilians not a hundred yards from him; an ambush that took—

The doors to the elevator swished open.

He trailed Julia to the main doors, picturing his empty house. "Would you like to go for a cup of coffee somewhere?"

She stopped and swung around, regret on her face. "I can't. A neighbor has been watching Ellie, but I need to get home and put her to bed." She tilted her head slightly to the side. "Where's Paige?"

"At Marge's, spending the night." *So I'll be alone with my thoughts.*

"I fix a great cup of coffee. Want to come to my place?"

Her invitation both surprised and elated him. "Yeah." Suddenly, the evening seemed less lonely.

Julia tucked Ellie into bed and kissed her before she tiptoed out of her daughter's room. When Evan had told her that Paige was at her grandmother's, she fought not to show how that affected her, but it was hard not to think about what Ellie and her mother were missing.

The scent of coffee wafted to her. She'd put it on when they had first arrived, then ushered her daughter down the hall to get ready for bed.

Julia entered the living room and came to a stop. Evan sat on her couch, relaxed, a parenting magazine open on his lap. When he flipped to the next page, he peered up. His gaze locked with hers.

"Great article on a child's first day of school." His mouth lifted in a lopsided grin. "Too bad I didn't see this before Paige started last August."

He seemed so at home in her apartment, it sent her heart beating fast. "Why? What happened?"

"She didn't want to leave the ranch. She hid from me, and it took me two hours to find her. Her first day became the second day."

"Ellie was the opposite. She pulled me up the walk to the building. I think she was lonely after moving here from Chicago and was eager to meet new friends." Julia crossed the room to the kitchen. "How do you like your coffee?"

"Strong and black."

She smiled and busied herself with fixing the drinks. Normally, she didn't prepare her coffee so strong, but for some reason she'd added an extra scoop for Evan. After doctoring hers with a little water and sugar, she headed back into the living room.

He scanned another article but put the magazine on the table in front of him when she handed him the mug. "I was surprised by Paige's behavior that day because usually she loves meeting new people."

"Did she already have any friends in the class?"

"A couple, but since Paige's mother died last winter she hasn't let me out of her sight for long. She's scared something is gonna happen to me. Lately she's been a lot better and will even spend the night at Marge's occasionally."

"How about over here?"

"I don't know."

"Ellie wants her to stay over one weekend. She mentioned something about it tonight before she conked out."

"We can ask Paige, but if she says no, don't take it personally. She just started going to Marge's house this past month. I think being at school all day has helped with her separation anxiety." He blew on his coffee.

"It sounds like you've taken her to counseling."

"Not long after I realized I was in over my head. Girls are different than boys."

"You think?"

"When I left the military, I was equipped to deal with soldiers, but my daughter was another story. The first year as a single dad was rocky, to say the least." He took a sip of his drink and sighed. "This is wonderful. You do make a great cup of joe."

"Don't sound so shocked. I am your cooking teacher." She sat at the other end of the couch. "I remember my first year as a single mom with a newborn. It was rough, especially since I had to finish my degree. I had a semester left." Julia drank from her mug, relishing the warmth after the chilly November evening. "Some of the hardest months of my life."

"What about your parents?"

She gripped the cup between her palms.

"Where do they live?"

"Chicago." She didn't want to go down this path, and yet she had opened the topic to conversation. Why? She never had before.

"Y'all lived in the same town and they didn't help you?"

"No. They wanted nothing to do with me or Ellie."

A frown crossed his face. "Why not?"

Her hands began to shake and she quickly placed the mug on the table so not to spill the coffee all over her. Nibbling on her lower lip, she studied the far wall and tried to come up with a way to answer his question without opening herself up to more pain.

"If you don't want to talk about it, I understand."

"Do you?" She still didn't look at him, afraid of what she might see in his expression. She didn't want anyone's pity.

His laughter sounded in the quiet, but there was no humor in it. "Believe me, I do. I have a past I don't like talking about."

A question concerning his deceased wife almost slipped out. Julia pressed her lips together and looked at him. "We could always talk about the weather."

After a long sip of his coffee, Evan rose. "I probably should be getting home. Tomorrow we'll need to be at the carnival early—me especially since I'm bringing most of the animals for the petting zoo."

Grateful that he really did understand, Julia pushed to her feet. "I could always bring Ellie's goldfish. Of course, it would probably be a little hard to pet."

"I think we'll have enough animals. That's not what I'm worried about."

"We could ban Taylor from the zoo."

"Not even him."

"Then what?"

"The weather." Evan grabbed another quick sip of his coffee, then handed the mug to Julia.

"Yes, I see where that could be a problem."

"Despite Olga's assurances it's not going to rain. It has been quite a bit lately."

"Then we will improvise."

"Ha! That's something I'm not very good at."

She leaned close to him and immediately regretted it. His fresh scent still teasing her nostrils, she pulled back and said, "Neither am I."

"Where's Paige? I haven't seen her here yet." Julia opened the gate to allow a little boy to go into the pen with four goats.

"Marge is bringing her, but she should have been here by now." Evan studied the stream of children and adults heading into the gym. "I'm glad Olga's prediction was right. There isn't a cloud in the sky."

"Mister—" a girl about six years old tugged on Evan's arm "—can I ride the pony?"

"Sure." Evan walked past Julia, pausing to whisper, "I hadn't planned on doing rides today. There isn't much room in this courtyard. Will you be okay by yourself?"

"Yes. I can open and close gates, no problem."

"I'll be over there. Whistle if you get into trouble."

She scoffed at that suggestion. These animals had been great with the children for the past hour since the carnival opened. She could handle a family of goats, two baby potbellied pigs, a sheep and two calves all in pens. She did draw the line with the boa that had hardly moved in his cage, probably because of the chill in the air.

For the next twenty minutes the petting zoo ran smoothly. A steady group of kids came through, but nothing too overwhelming. Julia relaxed against the post by the pigs' pen, watching two girls stroke the babies' backs.

"Julia, where's Ellie?"

She turned around to find Paige hurrying toward her with her grandma trailing behind her at a more sedate pace. "She's making the rounds of the booths inside. She's been looking for you."

"I'll go find her."

The child raced off, leaving Julia to face Marge by herself. "It's nice to see you again." She schooled her features into a smile.

Marge huffed, eyeing her as though she was reciting a list of Julia's flaws in her head. "Julie?"

"Julia." Nearly choking on the older

woman's scent of roses, Julia didn't offer her hand this time.

"I understand you are teaching my son-in-law how to cook."

Ice dripped off Marge's words and shivered through Julia. "Yes, he's doing quite well so far."

"I suppose cooking can be a type of therapy. After all that he has gone through, he certainly needs something to help him relax. My daughter's death affected him more than me." Marge heaved her purse higher on her arm and hugged it against her, shaking her head. "Poor boy."

"I'm sorry for your loss." Julia glanced toward Evan in the grass near the courtyard, leading Sugar around in a circle with a child on the pony's back, and thought about letting out a loud whistle. But would he even hear over the noise?

Marge stepped close and lowered her voice. "Let's quit playing the polite, little games. I won't let you come between my granddaughter and me or for that matter, between Evan and me. They are my family." Whirling about, moving faster than Julia thought possible, the woman stomped toward the entrance into the building.

Julia collapsed back against the post. Clasping her trembling hands together, she inhaled deep breaths, taking in the woman's overpowering perfume that lingered in the chilly air. She would have told Marge she wasn't in the market for a man, but she doubted the woman would have listened.

A whimper penetrated her thoughts. Julia spun toward the sound and saw a four-year-old trapped by goats in a pen. The child's parents didn't seem to be around, so she rushed inside, snatching some food Evan had brought for the animals in her haste.

She pushed her way through the goats—two large and two small ones—holding out her palms with the corn and seeds on them. The biggest one sniffed the air and made a beeline for her palm nearest it. Before she knew it, the other large one had her cornered with the two babies trying to inhale the food in the other palm.

"There you are. How did you get in here?" A mother hurried into the pen and scooped up her child who had stopped crying and was watching Julia.

As they left, Julia looked down at her hands and noticed the food was gone but the goats weren't. She tried to whistle but she barely heard the pitiful sound she made.

The largest goat tugged on her shirt. Another rubbed against her while a baby nibbled on the laces on her tennis shoe. Did goats bite? She did remember they liked to eat anything. Would she have holes in her clothes?

Pinned against the pen, her weight threatening to take the wire enclosure down, she peered up to see Evan. Wading through the goats, he managed to lure them away by scattering the corn and seeds on the ground on the other side. He held his hand out for her.

She fit hers within his and hastened for the gate. "Thanks." Leaning back against the post, she splayed her hand over her heart. "My, they are ferocious little animals when it comes to food."

"They do like to eat," Evan said with a chuckle. "I would have been here earlier but I had to finish the ride I had started. I saw Marge talking with you."

"Yes, we had a lovely little chat."

He raised an eyebrow. "Marge can be—territorial."

"Yes, and she has staked her claim."

"She thinks she will lose Paige if I marry again. I've tried to assure her nothing would change, that we're just friends anyway. She didn't believe me when I said I didn't want to get married again." Evan kneaded his nape. "And she doesn't think a man and woman can be friends."

If she were interested in any man romantically—which she wasn't—he would have to be a friend above anything. That was what she had wanted with Clayton. Whoa! How had she gone from being just friends to a marriage founded on deep friendship? The goat family must have rattled her more than she thought.

"We'll just have to prove Marge wrong, then I'm sure she will come around." Julia couldn't believe she had just said that. It wasn't as though she was hurting for friends. She had made quite a few in the short time she had come to Prairie Springs. She didn't need a man as a friend.

"She's a tough one, but for Paige I have to try to get her to understand."

What if she doesn't understand? Thankfully, she kept that question to herself. She had already put one foot in her mouth. She didn't need both of them in it.

When she caught sight of Paige and Ellie racing toward them, she sighed, applauding her child's perfect timing. "What are you guys up to?"

"We're hungry. Can we have some money for a hot dog?" Paige flipped her pigtails behind her shoulders.

"And some chips and pop?" Ellie scooted in front of Julia.

"Isn't there any good food in there?" Julia dug into her pocket for the money she had brought for their lunch.

"Hot dogs, chips and pop are good." Ellie held her palm out.

"I mean nutritious—good for your body."

Paige cocked her head to the side. "Why aren't they good for your body?"

Evan's laughter sprinkled the air. "Yeah, why not?"

The twinkle in his eyes made her laugh, too. "We don't have enough time to get into it here." She counted out some bills and gave them to Ellie.

"I can get some cotton candy, too." Paige took the money her dad handed her.

"Or an ice-cream cone." Ellie started to leave but stopped and turned back. "Can Paige spend the night with me tonight?"

Frowning, Paige looked at her father.

"How about you stay over at our house again?" Evan asked.

Paige beamed. "That would be great! How about it, Ellie?"

"But I want you to see my bedroom and toys."

"I'm sure I can even manage to give you a short riding lesson this evening." Evan threw Julia a pleading look for help.

"You're gonna be able to ride rings around me." Julia hooked Ellie's hair behind her ear.

"Okay. Let's go eat."

As the children ran off, Evan removed his cowboy hat and combed his fingers through his hair. "Thanks. I'm sure Paige will want to spend the night one day. But that doesn't stop me from worrying about her. She's so afraid something's gonna happen to me."

"Give her time. It heals a lot of wounds." She should know.

"Are you sure it's okay to come out to the barn like this?" Ellie asked Paige as they snuck out of the house and ran across the yard toward the brown structure.

"I come down here all the time. Dad doesn't care. I've been gone most of the weekend and miss Sugar and Bessie."

"Yeah, I wanted to ride last night. Too bad it was so late when we got here."

Paige tugged open the barn door and slipped inside. "Dinner was good. I liked the ice-cream sundae."

"So did I." Ellie hurried after her friend.

"I wish your mom could have come with us to get the sundaes."

"Yeah, then it would have been perfect. But she said she was tired and needed to get our laundry done if she was gonna spend this afternoon here." Drawn to the bay mare, Ellie made a beeline for Bessie.

"I like your mommy."

"I like your daddy."

In the middle of the barn Paige stopped and whirled around, her forehead wrinkled, her finger tapping against her chin. "I want a mommy."

"I've never had a daddy."

"Wouldn't it be great if we could be sisters?"

Ellie nodded. "We just need to get our parents together like in *The Parent Trap*." A whinny sound drew her attention. Bessie looked toward Ellie with big brown eyes and she completed her trek to the mare.

The horse hung her head out of the opened top part of the stall door. Paige came up beside Ellie. "She's my favorite."

"Mine, too," Ellie said, wishing she had her own horse like the mare. Bessie nudged Ellie's hand. She giggled. "She thinks I have something for her to eat."

"She's always looking for a treat. I know where Daddy keeps some sugar cubes. She has a sweet tooth."

Paige crossed to a room at the end of the stalls. When she returned, her friend opened the stall door and entered, motioning for Ellie to follow. She glanced around to make sure no one was around to see her, and then she slipped inside.

"This is how you do it. Lay your palm flat and put it near her mouth."

After Paige demonstrated, Ellie did as she was instructed. Bessie bent toward her and nibbled the sugar from her hand, tickling her. "She got it!"

The stall door creaked open. Ellie swept around expecting to see Paige's dad in the entrance. Instead a gray cat sauntered inside. Bessie ignored the animal as it weaved in and out of the horse's front legs.

"That's Mosey. They're friends." Paige produced another cube of sugar and presented it to the mare.

"Like us."

Suddenly a large, skinny white-and-black cat darted into the stall. Bessie backed up a few steps, dancing around.

"I've never seen that one." Paige pulled Ellie to the side.

The stray chased after Mosey, wanting to play. The mare snickered as if to give a warning to the strange cat. All Ellie could see was the animal getting hurt by the horse. She couldn't let that happen.

"We'd better get out of here." Paige sidled toward the open stall door.

Bessie reared up as the stray tried to wrestle with Mosey around her hooves. Without thinking, Ellie lunged toward the white-and-black animal to scoop it up, but in doing so she tripped and fell forward.

Just as Bessie came down.

Chapter Five

Julia dove across her bed to answer her phone on the nightstand. "Hello."

"Julia?"

The realization that her mother even had to ask if it was her on the line pierced through her heart. She didn't talk to her mom much anymore, but she would never forget her voice. "Yes, Mom. How are you doing?"

"Fine, honey. Is Ellie there? I wanted to talk to her."

"No, she's spending the night at a friend's."

"She's made friends already?"

It's been over four months. Of course your granddaughter has made friends. She gets along with everyone, and if you were around her, you would know that. The words were itching to come out, but she kept them locked away. "Yes. Lately Paige and Ellie have been inseparable."

"That's good she has a best friend. I'm not sure when I'll get to call back so I want to tell you that I'm coming for a few days for Ellie's birthday if that's all right with you."

If she hadn't been sprawled across her bed, she would have collapsed to the floor. "You are! When? How?"

"I'm flying down to Austin on Friday and returning here on Sunday."

"How about Dad? Is he there?"

"He went to the store. I'm gonna meet him in a little bit to have lunch downtown. Your father is going fishing out of town with some of his friends."

So when the cat's away, you decided to play—or rather be a grandmother for a change. "Okay. Do you want me to meet your plane in Austin?"

"No, I'm gonna rent a car and drive up to Prairie Springs. I should be there by midafternoon."

Did her mother want a way to escape fast if things didn't go well with her visit? Julia hated to think so, but it slipped through her defenses and bore into her. "Don't waste the money. I can pick you up."

"No. No, I just need directions to your apartment."

After Julia told her how to get to her place, her mother ended the conversation with, "I'll see you Friday. I need to leave soon."

So do I. Julia hung up and swung her legs to the floor. She started to stand, but the phone rang again. She quickly picked it up. "Julia, this is Evan."

The strain in his voice alerted her that something was wrong. "Is everything all right?"

"I sound that shook up?"

"Yes."

"One of our horses stomped Ellie's—"

"Oh, no!" She shot to her feet, then immediately sank back on the bed when all energy siphoned from her legs. "Are you taking her to the hospital? Is anything broken? Is she—"

"Hold on, Julia." A calm tone floated to her this time as though he were soothing a panicked horse. "I wanted to let you know about the accident, but Ellie is fine. She will have a bruised foot. I'm sure it's not broken. She's just scared. She—"

"I'll be right there."

She slammed the receiver down and ignored the blaring of the phone as she quickly snatched up her purse on her dresser and started for the front door. Halfway there she glanced down and noticed she was still in her pajamas. She retraced her steps and opened her closet to grab something to wear.

As she removed a shirt, she noticed her hand shaking. Ellie was her whole life. She didn't know what she would do if something happened to her. She had nothing besides her daughter.

Fifteen minutes later she was pushing the speed limit on Johnson Road and praying her tires held up this time. She intended to get new ones that week, but right now she didn't need another blowout. When she pulled onto the dirt road that led to Evan's house, she forced herself to relax and loosened her grip on the steering wheel.

Father, please let Ellie be okay. She's all I have.

She parked behind the house next to Evan's truck and scrambled out of the car. The second her feet touched the back stoop, the door swung open and Evan filled the entrance. Worry scored his features and heightened her fear.

"Why did you come all the way out here? Everything's all right." The worry dissolved into an exasperated look. "She's not crying any—"

Julia pushed past him into the kitchen and scanned the area. "Where's Ellie?"

"With Paige back in her bed—"

Julia crossed to the hallway and rushed down it. The sound of laughter slowed her pace, easing some of her anxiety. When she stepped into Paige's room, the girls sat on the floor playing a variation of Memory, matching different animal cards.

Ellie peered up at her and frowned. "Why are you here, Mommy?"

"Evan called me about your accident. I came to check on you and see if I need to take you to the doctor." As she spoke, her voiced lowered to almost a whisper when she took in how healthy and happy her daughter appeared. "He said you were crying."

Ellie finished her turn, flipping over a card of a horse that didn't match the pig she had already chosen. Then she rose and walked toward Julia without limping. Her daughter threw her arms around her. "I'm fine. I was scared at first. The cat spooked Bessie and she got scared, but she can't cry when she's scared."

Julia leaned back and peered down at her daughter. "Are you sure you're all right?"

Ellie stepped back and pointed toward her

foot. "Evan says I'll probably have a bruise where Bessie's hoof grazed me."

"Grazed you?" Julia knelt and took off Ellie's sock to check for herself. Her skin had started to turn a bluish red color. "Then nothing's broken?"

"No. See?" Ellie said and pranced around the bedroom. "I can walk fine."

Julia stood, aware of Evan in the doorway. Perhaps she had overreacted. Maybe she should have listened to Evan explain everything before rushing out here. She had struggled so much the past six years—raising Ellie by herself, finishing school, paying off her debts—that she was the one who was scared. This move to Prairie Springs seemed to be an answer to her prayers—a good place to raise her daughter where they would be accepted for who they were. Her mother's call had momentarily plunged her back into the past, into her guilt and doubts.

Backing out of the room, Julia motioned with her hand. "Go on and finish the game. I'll be with Evan in the kitchen." Apologizing, she silently added, the nerves along her spine tingling. He was still behind her, probably upset with her.

When she finally turned, the hallway was empty. Her stomach rumbled as she strode toward the kitchen. She hadn't even had her first cup of coffee yet.

As if Evan could read her mind, he filled his coffeepot with water and proceeded to make some. She slinked to the table and sat. He didn't face her until the aroma of the brew mocked her—"see what you could have had if you had stayed home?"

"Are you satisfied now your daughter is all right? Like I said."

"Yes," she murmured, refusing to look away from him although the urge was strong. "I'm sorry. I overreacted. All I heard were the words *horse* and *stomped* and my mind shut down. Now that I'm calm, I can listen to what happened."

"The girls snuck out of the house early and went to the barn to see the horses. Paige knows better than to go into a stall without me or another adult, but they did and somehow a stray cat spooked Bessie. Ellie was trying to save the cat and the mare grazed her. You saw for yourself she is fine?"

Julia nodded. During his explanation he had kept a strained if polite expression on his face, which only made her feel worse. If there was one thing she had discovered about Evan in the short time she'd known him it was that he was a good father. "This morning really didn't have anything to do with you. You are a great father. Paige is blessed to have you."

He moved to the table and leaned into it with the flat of his hands on the wooden top. "Then what is it about?"

The coffee finished perking. "May I have a cup? I haven't had any yet."

After taking an extra mug down from the cabinet, he poured some for her and then filled his cup, which was sitting by the sink. He brought hers to the table and sat across from her. "Then what is it?" he repeated.

"My mother called this morning. She's coming next weekend for Ellie's birthday on Saturday."

"That's wonderful. I'm sure Ellie will be happy to see her."

"It will be one of the few times she has," Julia said, then sipped her coffee, seeking the warmth to melt the chill gripping her as she recalled her phone conversation with her mother.

"Really?"

"Yes, and to answer your next question, my mother never wanted to see Ellie much before this because my parents disowned me when I became pregnant with Ellie. I guess to really be fair, I should say my father disowned me and my mother felt she had to go along with him."

For a long moment silence hovered over the kitchen. Slowly, she became aware that the wall clock ticked and the girls were laughing and talking.

"I'm sorry, Julia. That couldn't have been easy for you." Evan picked up his mug, his gaze riveted to hers over the rim. "If your mother is coming to see Ellie, does that mean your father has changed his mind?"

"He'll be on a fishing trip, and Mom will be coming without him knowing, which in itself is surprising to me. They share everything." She ran her finger around the top of her mug. "I know God has forgiven me, and I can accept that my father never will, but I hate seeing Ellie hurt by it. She's the innocent in all this."

"It's hard watching our children hurting."

"I'm almost afraid to be alone with Mom. Aren't mothers supposed to protect and love their children no matter what?"

"You don't think yours has?"

The wounds inflicted by her parents remained open and festering. Tears, she'd thought she had completely shed, began to well up. She dropped her head, squeezing her eyes closed.

But she couldn't stop them. First one, then another fell.

Evan slipped his arm around her and pressed her against his side. She didn't usually cry, and especially not in the arms of a man she had only known for a short time. His hand stroked her back as though that action could take the hurt away. And for a few seconds, it did. She and Clayton had been together three years, and yet in this moment she felt closer to Evan than she ever had with Clayton.

"What can I do to help you, Julia?"

His whispered question enveloped her, as if he would take on the world for her. No one had ever made her feel that way. It awed her.

She pulled back and stared into his face. "Trade places with me next weekend?"

"I don't think I would fool your mother," he said with amusement, still holding her close.

"I'm sure I could find you a wig somewhere." She responded with a smile.

"I do have a suggestion. Why don't you have Ellie's birthday party out here at the ranch? The children could ride the horses, we could have a mini rodeo for them, a clown included, and then finish with a barbecue. What do you say?"

She threw her arms around his neck and

kissed him on the cheek. As she drew back, heat flamed her face at her impulsive act.

"I take it that is a 'yes'?"

"You've got yourself a birthday party, but—" Julia peered over her shoulder toward the hallway "—I want it to be a surprise. I'll tell Ellie we're coming out here for a riding lesson on Saturday. Do you think Paige can keep the secret?"

"She won't know about it until that morning. She wouldn't intend to tell. It would just come out. I always know what she has made me for my birthday and Christmas."

At that moment her stomach decided to rumble its hunger again. Evan laughed. "I have some cereal if you want. Or…" Evan rose and put the chair he was sitting in back where it belonged, then made his way to the refrigerator. "While I was buying the ingredients for the pizza, I also picked up some other items. I have the makings of a turkey sandwich in here. Want one?"

When he opened the fridge to reveal its contents, Julia attempted a whistle that didn't do much better than the one the day before. "I'm impressed. You actually have food on those shelves."

"You just wait until I get you up on a horse this afternoon. I'll have my revenge." He winked.

* * *

Evan's revenge had to be that parts of her body she hadn't realized she had were aching. Julia shifted, but still her bottom impacted hard with the leather saddle each step her mare took.

"Uncle," Julia called out to Evan's back.

He angled around on his horse, one hand on its rump, and arched a brow.

"Uncle? Mommy, you are so funny," Ellie said from behind her on the trail.

Yeah, any moment now she was going to go on the road with her comedy act. "I'm not funny. I'm hurting."

"We've only been partway around the ranch." Evan faced forward again.

"Partway! We've been riding—" Julia checked her watch "—forty minutes. Just how big is this place?"

"I wanted to show you a special place. Another five or ten minutes."

It was *ten* minutes later when Julia's horse halted by the stream. She swung her leg over the saddle and crumpled to the ground in a heap.

Evan held a hand out for her. Pulling her up to her feet, he steadied her until she said, "I'm okay. I can feel my legs now. I'm just grateful you've got a horse that likes to follow yours.

Otherwise, I'm afraid I would still be back at that last patch of tall grass she discovered. You would think as many times as she paused to eat that you don't feed your animals."

"Walk around. That will help."

His smug expression pricked her. "You're enjoying yourself too much."

"I imagine you'll get me back when you try to show me how to make pizza. I have been studying up on some cooking terms. I know what *braise* means."

"Excellent. A pot roast would be a nice dish to teach you."

"That sounds complicated."

"You think boiling water is complicated."

"True." Evan peered beyond her. "Paige, don't go into the water. It's fifty degrees."

"There's a stone path across the stream." His daughter gestured toward it.

"Those stones are slippery, and I don't want a little girl getting wet when she falls in."

Paige crossed her arms and set her mouth in a pout. Ellie mimicked her friend.

"Can I show Ellie where the spring comes out of the rocks?" Paige finally asked when she didn't get any reaction from Evan.

"Only if you promise you won't go into the

water, which means to stand back from the edge. One accident in a day is all I want to handle."

Her daughter lowered her head and stared at the ground. Paige nodded, then motioned for Ellie to follow her.

"Shouldn't we go with them?"

"In a sec. The stream isn't deep at this time of year." He waited until the girls were out of earshot. "I wanted to ask you if I could give Ellie the cat she 'saved' this morning."

"Why?" A cat! That was a *real* pet. A goldfish really didn't count.

"Because after lunch when we were in the barn, she asked me if she could look for it and take it home. She didn't want it to get hurt when she wasn't there to look after it."

"Ah. I didn't realize she loved animals so much."

"Most children do when given the chance."

She chewed on her bottom lip. "A cat isn't like a dog?"

"Definitely different animals."

"They can be kept in a small apartment and be happy?"

"The last time I checked with one, yes."

Although he was teasing her, she kept a serious expression because if Ellie fell in love with the cat and something happened to it, then—was she really talking about her daughter here? Or was it that she was afraid of loving something and getting hurt again?

"The cat's a stray. What if it runs away?"

"Most likely if you feed her, she'll stay. She's thin, which means she's been on her own for a while, but the way she has responded to the girls, I'm thinking she's had a family at one time."

"Can we take her on Saturday then? Will you keep her until then?"

"Yeah." Evan began walking toward where the girls were.

"I'll need to pick up supplies and food. I'll need to get a book about cats. I'll need—"

"To stop stressing about having a pet. It will work itself out. Feed and love it. That usually works well."

"This from a man who has so many animals he probably doesn't even know how many."

He chuckled. "Not true. Not counting the cattle, which I do know exactly how many, unless one was born today unexpectedly, I have thirty-six animals on the ranch."

A man who likes to be in control of his environment. Like me. "Okay, then humor me. I like to know about what I'm doing before I plunge right in."

"Most people do, but what do you do when something just drops in your lap?"

"Scream and run?" The kids came into view, and Julia slowed her step, angling toward him. "I'm learning about going with the flow. I just don't have the hang of it yet."

"For years I've tried to make my life go a certain way, but it has a mind of its own. There was a time I thought I would make the army my career, then retire to Texas and live on a ranch. Life intruded and I had to change my plans."

"You didn't exactly change your plans, just altered the timing a little."

He stopped and faced her. "A little? I'd say twenty-two years is a big change."

"Why did you feel you had to change?"

His gaze swept toward Paige. "For her. It's hard enough to be a single father, let alone be in the army, deployed in a war zone. Or at least it was for me."

"What happened?" Julia asked, aware she was treading in an area that was very personal, which could take their casual friendship to a whole new level. Wasn't it already after her confession about her mother earlier?

"My wife walked away from Paige and our marriage on Thanksgiving two years ago. I have to admit that it isn't my favorite holiday."

Julia glimpsed at both girls planting themselves on a fallen log. They bent their heads close together and talked. "She left Paige alone?"

"My daughter was staying with Diane's mother the night before Thanksgiving. Diane was supposed to come over that morning and help with preparing the food. She never showed up. Instead, a few hours later she called her mother and told her she was getting on a plane for California."

Laughter echoed through the small glade. The two girls did a high five and then continued to chatter with occasional peeks at Evan and her. Clearly the children were discussing them. She made a decision to have her own talk with Ellie. She didn't want her daughter to wish for something that just wasn't going to be.

Julia swung her attention back to Evan. "You were overseas at that time?"

"Yes. Marge didn't let me know what had happened for a few days. And the only reason I found out at the time I did was because Paige told me. I knew then I couldn't stay in the army. Marge loves my daughter, but I had to raise her myself. I left the army early and settled in Prairie Springs so Paige wouldn't be yanked away from everything familiar to her."

"Diane didn't want Paige with her in California?"

"No way. A little girl would have interfered with her career in Hollywood." Sarcasm tainted each word as a scowl molded his features.

"I'm so sorry."

"The worst part about it was that Diane didn't want to have anything to do with Paige. She talked to her daughter four times in fifteen months and sent her a Christmas present that first year she was gone. Nothing for the second—" he coughed and swallowed several times, as though sadness jammed his throat "—Christmas or either of her birthdays. Paige's own mother rejected her, and she knew it."

"Then I know how she feels." Julia's heart cracked, feeling the child's pain as if it were her own.

Evan turned his back on the two girls. "How can a mother walk out on her child?"

Talk to mine. She might be able to tell you. Paige wanted to say those words, but in all fairness her mother hadn't completely cut off all ties. "What did Diane tell you?"

"Not much. She'd always wanted to be an actress, and she knew her time was running out. She wasn't getting any younger and had to do something *now*." Evan shook his head. "What a cliché. I didn't know people ran off to Hollywood anymore."

"There are still some people who dream of having a glamorous life like a movie star. Did she act in high school?"

"No, but she did do some modeling. She was a very beautiful woman." The word beautiful came out as though it was a dirty word. "I know the Lord wants me to forgive Diane, but I'm having a hard time with that. Have you forgiven your parents?"

This was her chance to bare her soul to Evan, and yet his question stunned her because she hadn't really faced the issue. Had she forgiven her parents? She looked into her heart and realized she hadn't. Anger dwelled there when she thought about her mother and father. She always disguised it as feeling upset because of what they had done to Ellie. But that wasn't all of it. She was furious at what they had also done to *her*.

"No, I haven't." She stared at Evan, all barriers between them crumbled for these few minutes of shared pain. She never felt so close to another as in that moment. "And I'm not sure I can."

"Then you have your doubts about your faith?"

"No, I don't have doubts. I'm just having a hard time doing what the Lord wants me to do. I know Jesus forgave the people who sinned against him, but I'm not perfect. I don't know if I can."

"Then we are alike."

Yes, they were alike in a lot of ways. Those similarities made talking to Evan so easy. When she'd moved to a new town, she'd left behind her friends and she'd missed them. Slowly she was making new ones here, but the support system she'd had in Chicago wasn't in place yet. She'd never had a male friend like Evan.

"Mommy," Ellie shouted. Her daughter hopped off the log and ran toward her. "Me and Paige have a great idea!"

"What?" Sighing, Julia knelt and clasped Ellie's arm while Paige skidded to a halt behind her daughter.

"We've been talking about the soldiers in the Middle East in class. Ya know, about the Wall of Hope we helped with. Well, we decided—" Ellie pointed to Paige then herself "—we want to do something more."

"But we don't know what." Paige peered up at her dad. "Can you help us?"

"Oh, let's see." Evan stared off into space, rubbing his hand along the back of his neck. "They can always use letters from home."

"We don't write too well, Daddy."

"They can always use things like shampoo and deodorant. Items like that." Julia rose.

"I have three dollars saved," Ellie said.

"I have five dollars." Paige's eyebrows crunched into a thoughtful expression. "Will that buy much?"

"A couple of things." Evan slid a glance toward Julia.

Her face beaming, Ellie jumped up and down. "I've got it. Let's raise money for the soldiers."

Paige rested her elbow on her arm folded across her chest, cupping her face. "Hmm. How?" Suddenly her eyes widened. "I've got it! We can sell hot chocolate at the parade next week."

"I like it!" Ellie gave Paige a high five.

Julia thought of all the problems involved and almost said something until she saw the joy on the girls' faces. "The parade on Veterans Day? That would be a great time to have it. What do you think, Evan?"

He smiled. "I know the perfect place we can

have it. I'll call Reverend Fields and see if we can set a stand up out front on the church lawn. I'm sure he'll say yes. Julia, if you take care of the hot chocolate, I'll take care of the rest— talking with the reverend, the stand itself, even a little advertising."

As the girls danced about, their excitement contagious, Julia threw back her head and let the sun bathe her face. This would give her something to concentrate on instead of her problems with her mother and her impending visit.

Chapter Six

Pacing from the couch to the window that overlooked the street, Julia glanced at her watch. She pushed the sheer curtain to the side and peered outside. Mom was late. She probably changed her mind and didn't get on the airplane. This was the reason she hadn't said anything to her daughter about her mother coming to visit. She hadn't wanted to get Ellie's hopes up and then have them dashed.

Maybe she had dreamed the phone call from her mother. It had seemed so unreal after she had hung up. Mom had never gone against her father.

Spinning around, she strode back to the couch, staring down at the blue-and-brown plaid pattern. She needed to call Evan and tell him she would be late picking up Ellie. She had to give her mother another hour before she left for the ranch.

With a grip on the receiver, she punched in his number. When Evan answered on the third ring, she said, "She isn't here yet. I need to stay here for a while longer before coming to get Ellie."

"Have you heard from her? Was the plane late?"

The sound of his deep Texan drawl soothed her. "I haven't spoken to her since last weekend. I don't know which flight she took. Frankly, I don't think she's coming. This wouldn't be the first time she changed her mind. One other time when we lived in Chicago, she had planned to come see Ellie, but then Dad didn't go fishing, so she didn't come." That time she had told Ellie her grandma was coming to visit. Her daughter's confusion and tears had mirrored her own.

"I'm sorry, Julia. We can talk when you get here."

"Thanks. Bye."

All she wanted to do was leave and head for the ranch. A picture of Evan holding her formed in her mind and gave her comfort. But she wanted the real thing. He understood what she was going through.

Mom, you have half an hour.

She couldn't remain idle while she waited. She would go crazy. Deciding to load the trunk with items for Ellie's birthday party tomorrow, she made her way into the kitchen where she had the food on the table in bags and boxes. After gathering the sacks of cookies, a cake and sandwiches, she started for the front door.

The bell chimed. She checked the peephole and saw her mother in the hallway. "Just a minute."

With a quick look around her, she scooted back to the coffee table and stacked the boxes on it, then opened the door to see her mother. Sweat beaded Julia's forehead, and her chest tightened as she and her mother stared at each other.

"It's good to see you, Julia." Tears welled in her mom's eyes.

They pricked her defenses. But then Julia remembered the pain she and Ellie had gone through, especially the last time she was supposed to visit, and toughened her resolve. She was afraid to trust this unexpected change of heart.

Julia stepped to the side. "Come in. You're late and I was about to leave." Wincing at the almost harsh tone to her words, she forced a small smile to her lips. "That is, I have to pick Ellie up soon."

"She isn't here?"

"She went home with a friend after school." It worked out well, she thought, since she hadn't wanted her daughter there when her mother arrived—if she arrived. Julia grabbed her mother's suitcase and brought it into the apartment.

Her mom scanned the place. "Nice."

What did you expect—a hovel? Julia bit her lower lip to keep the words inside. She gestured toward the boxes. "I was taking those out to my car. I'm having Ellie's birthday party at Paige's tomorrow."

"Paige?"

"The friend from school. She lives on a ranch and her father offered to have the party there. You know how much Ellie loves horses. Sorry, maybe you don't." Closing her eyes, Julia counted to ten.

This reunion wasn't starting out well at all, which was one of the reasons she hadn't wanted her daughter here to witness it. If she couldn't get past her anger, this would be a tension-filled weekend.

Lord, I don't know if I have it in me. Please show me the way. I'm lost as to what to do.

"That's lovely that Paige's father offered to host the party at the ranch. I imagine Ellie is excited," her mother said in a stiff, polite voice, her body ramrod straight, her hands clutching her brown leather purse in front of her, as if it were a shield to protect her from Julia's barbs.

The thought brought Julia up short. This wasn't easy for her mother, either. "Ellie doesn't know. It's to be a surprise tomorrow."

"I see, then she won't hear about it from me."

"Thanks. I appreciate that. You can help by carrying some of the party supplies out to the car. I'm taking most of it out there tonight so I don't have to tomorrow."

"How are you going to unload the car without your daughter seeing you?"

"You wait." A smile wavered at the corners of Julia's mouth. "Ellie's in her own world when she is around horses. I'm just waiting for her to ask me for one for Christmas. The highlight of her week is her riding lesson."

"She's learning to ride?" Astonishment sounded in her mother's voice.

"Evan's a great teacher. She's doing better than I am." It had taken days for her not to ache after that ride around his ranch last Sunday.

"You're taking lessons, too?" Her mother's mouth set in a frown. "You never liked animals much."

"What makes you say that?"

"You never talked about them."

"Because I could never have a pet. I found other things to care about."

"Your dad was allergic to cats and dogs."

"There were other pets I could have had."

The frown on her mother's face deepened. "Where should I take my suitcase?"

"You'll stay in Ellie's room. She'll sleep with me. I'll take it in there."

Julia scurried from the living room, needing to get away from her mother for a moment before the anger she was trying to forget exploded from her lips. She felt as if she were a teenager again and couldn't meet her mother's expectations. Disapproval was in her mother's every word.

And yet she'd come to see Ellie. Julia had to remember that and prayed the weekend went well for her daughter's sake.

After depositing the luggage in Ellie's bedroom, Julia flipped her cell phone open and punched in Evan's number, now on her speed-dial list.

"Mom's here. We're coming out to the ranch now."

"The kids will be down at the barn. One of my ranch hands will keep them busy while we empty your trunk."

"Great. Everything all right?"

"Yep. I've been delaying them and having to listen to their whining. You owe me big-time."

"I know. This will be the best birthday party Ellie's ever had."

"Oh, how many has she had?"

"One. Last year. But I'm sure when she's older and looks back on this one, she'll feel that way."

His laughter bathed her in warmth. "See you in a while."

Julia pocketed her cell and entered the living room again. Her mother stood before her bookcase, inspecting its contents.

"I see you still read romances." The censure in her mom's voice further heightened Julia's strain.

"Yes, my tastes are the same. I have expanded into reading suspense and thrillers, though."

She snorted. "I prefer nonfiction."

"Let's go." Julia crossed to the front door, grabbed her purse from the table next to it and went out to the car.

Patience and tolerance. She needed both to survive the next couple of days.

"This is a nice town. Not too large. Chicago is getting so big," her mother said when Julia drove down Veterans Boulevard, the main street in Prairie Springs.

"The town revolves around the army base. Veterans Day will be a big deal next week. Ellie and Paige came up with a fund-raiser to help the troops. They'll sell hot chocolate during the parade."

"By themselves?" she asked with surprise lacing her voice.

"Evan and I will be near to help, but they want to do it by themselves."

"Who is this Evan you keep mentioning?"

"Paige's dad."

"And his wife? Where is she?"

"She died earlier this year."

"Are you dating him, a man whose wife hasn't even been in the grave a year?"

The disapproval thickened Julia's throat. She swallowed several times before she managed to say, "We are friends. That's all."

"Friends with a man?"

"It does happen, Mom. His daughter is a friend of Ellie's. We have quite a bit in common."

She snorted. "Have you forgotten Clayton?"

Heat scored Julia's cheeks. "No, I haven't forgotten Ellie's father."

"Do you want something like *that* to happen again?"

"I've learned from my mistakes." Julia

clamped her lips together to keep from saying anything else.

Silence charged the air, but Julia wouldn't break it for the world.

When she turned onto the road that led to Evan's, her mother sat up straight, her hands clasped together in her lap so tightly that her fingertips reddened.

"Ellie doesn't have a name for me yet. I want to be called Nana."

"Fine, Mom. I'll say something to Ellie." Had her mother really thought this visit would be a good idea?

Evan's house came into view. Some of the stress in Julia diminished when she saw him standing on his porch, gesturing for her to park in front, rather than in the back.

"I take it that's your Evan."

"He isn't mine. But it is Evan."

Julia clambered from her car so quickly she almost stumbled into Evan's arms as he approached. She stepped back before her mother drew the wrong conclusion and had a chance to continue their earlier awkward conversation.

"Okay?" he whispered as he skirted her and headed straight for the other side. Evan opened the car door for her mother and tipped his cowboy hat. "I've been looking forward to meeting you, Mrs. Saunders. Welcome to Texas."

Her mother shook his hand. "You have a nice place. It's big."

"Not by Texan standards, ma'am."

She pointed toward the river running through his property on the east. "What's it called?"

"That's the Prairie Spring River. I like to sit on my front porch in the early morning and drink my first cup of coffee. Watching the water flow by with the sun coming up is a great way to start my day." He gave her a dimple-producing grin. "Was your flight all right?"

"Horrible. Plastic-tasting food, and the flight was late arriving."

"I'm sorry to hear that." He regarded Julia over the top of her green Mustang. "Is everything in your trunk?"

"Yes, we'd better get these bags inside before Ellie catches us."

"We'll put them in my bedroom closet. That's where I usually hide Paige's presents and she hasn't found them yet." After Julia popped the trunk, he loaded his arms with boxes and sacks and led the way.

Quickly, Julia and her mother followed suit, emptying the car in one trip. When Julia crossed the threshold into his room, the first thing she noticed was how masculine it was. Heavy oak furniture took up most of the space from his four-poster bed with a solid navy blue coverlet to the two nightstands, a desk and chair and an armoire. The only thing that didn't fit was the large antique trunk with brass fixtures at the foot of the bed.

After passing her load to Evan, her mother motioned toward the trunk. "That's beautiful. A family heirloom?"

"Yes, how did you guess?" Evan winked at Julia as her mom examined the piece.

"It looks old but well kept."

"It's the only thing of my mother's family I have. I hope to pass it on to Paige when she leaves home."

Her mother glanced back at him as if she was reassessing him. "I hope she'll appreciate it."

"She will. She already wants me to move it into her room, but I'm gonna wait a few more years before I do." Evan put his hand at the small of Julia's back. "Let's go see what the girls are up to. If they have done what Buddy planned for them, they should have a stall cleaned by now."

"Ellie's cleaning out dirty stalls? Isn't she

a little young to be doing that?" Her mother sent Evan a sharp look that would have silenced any other man.

"If you're learning to ride a horse, you need to learn to take care of it, too. I'm even teaching her to brush and groom Bessie."

"A full-grown horse?"

"Yes. Ellie and Paige use a stool to help them do a proper job."

Her mother gave Julia the same sharp gaze, cutting right through her. "I don't know about this. It can't be safe. Ellie is only five."

"She'll be six tomorrow, Mom. Please don't say anything about the riding to her. This is between my daughter and me."

"Fine." Her mother snapped her mouth closed, her gaze trained forward.

The sympathy in Evan's eyes calmed Julia. But even more than that, she could see in his expression that he knew exactly what she was going through. That connection between them gave her the strength to continue with her mother.

"Paige. Ellie," Evan called out when they entered the barn.

His daughter popped her head out of a middle stall. "Almost finished, Daddy."

"A lady is here with your mommy," Paige could be heard saying in the stall.

Ellie emerged, hay sticking out of her hair, dirt on her knees and white shirt. "We aren't through yet. And Evan said we could ride if we did a good job." Ellie's gaze swung to Julia's mother. Ellie tilted her head to the side and studied the woman.

"Honey, this is Nana, your grandmother." Julia noted on her mother the shorter hair, which was almost totally gray now. Although Ellie had seen some photos of her, it had been almost three years since she had seen her in real life.

A stunned expression descended on Ellie's face, her mouth falling opening, her eyes round.

Maybe she should have prepared her daughter for her grandmother's visit. Then she remembered the last time, the sound of the sobs coming from her daughter's bedroom, and knew she had been right to wait.

"I flew all the way down here just so I could be here for your birthday tomorrow." With tears in her eyes, her mother covered the distance to Ellie and placed her hands on her grand-daughter's shoulders. "You look so much more grown-up than the picture you sent me last summer. You are getting so big."

Ellie beamed. "I grew two inches this year."

"And your hair is longer." Her mother turned Ellie around. "But I like it like this."

Evan came up behind Julia and leaned close. "I think it's going all right."

"Better than I imagined." Her hoarse words clogged her throat, his presence fortifying her more than he would ever know.

Did her mom really care about Ellie? Was there some reason behind this visit?

"Nana, what's wrong? You're crying. Did you hurt yourself?"

"No, I'm just glad to be able to hold you again."

Julia spun around to face Evan. "I think something happened to my mom when she came through your barn doors. What did you do with my real mother?"

"How can she resist Ellie's smile? She can charm anyone." He tossed his head toward the two still standing in front of the stall.

Maybe she should take lessons from her daughter, because Julia's relationship with her mother wasn't anything like what she was witnessing between Ellie and her grandmother.

Paige peered around the barn door then leaped back. "She's coming. Hide, everyone."

Kids scattered so fast that Evan's head spun.

"Daddy, you, too," Paige called out from her hiding place in the tack room.

Where? Every place was taken with children from Ellie's class along with a few adults. He found an unoccupied area in Bessie's stall.

"Mommy, where's Paige and Evan?"

The sound of Ellie's voice triggered the kids into action. First Paige, then five more and finally ten others popped up and yelled, "Surprise!"

Shock flashed across Ellie's face, then the biggest smile Evan had seen on her, so far. She ran into the mob of kids massing in the center of the barn. "You're here for my birthday party?"

"Were you surprised? I had to keep the secret *all* morning." Paige hopped up and down, energy pouring off her.

When he had told Paige, she'd glanced at the phone, and he could see her thinking through whether she could sneak into the other room to make a call to Ellie. If he could have set up the party without informing his daughter, he would have. Instead, he put her to work and kept her so busy she didn't have time to think about calling her best friend.

While Paige gave the children from her class

a tour and showed them all the animals, Caitlyn Villard and Steve Windham approached him. "I'm glad you could help us out with chaperoning."

"My nieces have been dying all week to come out here. They can't wait to ride." Caitlyn took Steve's hand.

"This is a huge success, Evan. Thanks for offering to host the party." Julia joined them while Mrs. Saunders stayed in the middle of the kids.

"Your mother is a brave soul," Caitlyn said and smoothed her tousled hair behind her ear.

"She's hardly left Ellie's side," Julia said, with visible dark circles under her tired eyes.

The urge to comfort Julia inundated Evan. This visit with her mom was taking its toll. He knew what she was going through. When Marge would leave his house, exhaustion would always claim him.

"It's nice that she could be here for your daughter's birthday." Steve slipped his arm around Caitlyn who snuggled closer.

Seeing his friends' love so evident in their expressions for each other, created a yearning in Evan that slowed his heartbeat to an aching throb. That was all he'd ever wanted when he had married Diane, but she had betrayed their love.

He could still remember exactly where he had been when he'd received the call from Marge to inform him what Diane had done on Thanksgiving. He'd been on patrol and had only returned to camp a couple of hours before. The call had left him stunned and confused. He'd talked to Diane and Paige a few days before and there hadn't been a hint that there was a problem. He'd even told her he was coming home for Christmas. It hadn't made any difference in the long run.

Why hadn't he seen it coming?

In combat he'd needed to be prepared for surprises. In the rest of his life he'd worked hard not to have to deal with them. He still tried to control as much of his life as possible and falling in love meant giving up control over his emotions. He'd done it once. He didn't want to do it again.

His ranch hand waved to him from the entrance. He nodded, then said to the kids who had completed their tour, "We've got a rodeo for y'all and we're gonna need some help with it. Anyone want to be a clown?"

Ten hands shot up in the air.

Evan pointed to a boy and a girl. "I want you to go with Buddy. He's gonna get you ready. Now, I need three more people who will barrel race."

Ellie jumped up and down with Josie next to her. Reluctantly, a tall boy raised his arm. Evan motioned for another ranch hand to take the girls and boy and help them get ready.

Julia touched his arm. "Barrel racing? Isn't that a little advanced for these kids?"

"Not on what I have for them to use. I borrowed a stubborn donkey from my neighbor. It only knows one speed—slow—if it even goes that fast."

Julia relaxed her tense shoulders. Her fingers began to slide off his arm when he captured her hand and held it to him.

"Trust me."

She nodded, squeezed his arm, then moved away. He missed her touch.

Quickly, Evan went through the list of the rest of the events for the rodeo until every child had something to do. He started with the three children who were going to rope a calf.

Steve stopped him. "Can I have a word with you?"

Evan turned back to the base chaplain. The look on his friend's face quickened his pulse. "You've heard something about Whitney."

"Possibly. Your old unit is checking into a rumor about a couple who was kidnapped and are being held in the north. I know that John was found, but he had been wandering around that area when the patrol discovered him. Maybe he got away and went for help."

"Kidnapped? John wouldn't have left Whitney." Evan gripped the post nearby to steady himself. If only his brother-in-law remembered what happened. He kept hoping one day he would get a call informing him John had recovered his memory and knew exactly where Whitney was.

"It's just a rumor. They are checking out everything."

"This not knowing is killing me. If Whitney was kidnapped, I can't even…" The words couldn't get past the lump in his throat.

"Our Father will bring your sister home to you."

"Yeah, but how? In a body bag?" Evan pivoted and hurried to the waiting children.

He couldn't think about it now, or he would ruin Ellie's birthday party. He wouldn't do that to the little girl or to Julia. But the thought of his little sister held captive chilled his blood.

Looking around at all Evan had done for her daughter today swelled her heart, but Julia sensed something was wrong. She wanted to hold him, make whatever it was that was bothering him go away.

The rodeo was a big hit, and all the children were grinning from ear to ear. No one had ever done anything like this for her, and she wouldn't forget it.

"The last event is the barrel racing. I watched the ranch hand work with Ellie and the other children, using a pony. He told them they would each ride the same animal and the one who had the best time would win." Her mother chuckled. "But Evan told me what they don't know is that the animal isn't a pony but a donkey that hardly moves. So it's safe. I was worried but that young man of yours took his time to explain what would happen."

Julia started to correct her mother. Evan wasn't her young man, but at that moment he had motioned for the crowd to be quiet, then he disappeared into the barn.

A few seconds later he pulled a dark gray donkey out into the paddock where the barrels were set several feet apart. Josie held the reins, her back straight. When he stepped away and signaled the race had begun by waving a white handkerchief, the little girl urged the donkey forward. But it didn't budge. For three minutes she tried while all the kids laughed and shouted encouragements. Finally she got off the animal, took the reins and led it around the barrels. The audience clapped at her quick thinking.

The boy came out next and tried his hand at barrel racing. The animal took two steps and the crowd went wild with cheering. Suddenly, it looked toward the children and stopped. The boy bounced up and down a couple of times, trying to get it to respond. Finally, he gave up and sat on it until his time ran out.

Then Ellie rode the stubborn donkey into the ring where it headed in the opposite direction of the barrels. A big clown and a small one ran out into the ring and waved their arms madly, trying to maneuver the animal back toward the barrels. Someone opened the corral gate and the donkey kept plodding forward, right out of the paddock. The big clown chased after them and caught up with the pair, making a production out of blocking their way.

Laughter filled the crisp fall air. Finally Ellie slid off its back and took a bow, sweeping her arm across her body as if she had orchestrated the whole routine.

Julia glanced at her mother. Tears of merriment ran down her cheeks. Their gazes linked. Years of separation fell away in that moment. Julia wound her arms around her mom and hugged her.

A loud clanging disturbed the air. The crowd grew silent, trying to locate the source of the sound.

"The food is on," Evan said, pointing toward some tables set up outside behind his house.

Ellie ran up to Julia and threw her arms around her. "This is the best day I've ever had. Thank you, Mommy."

"I couldn't have done it without Evan. You need to thank him." She brushed her daughter's hair back from her face.

"I will, Mommy." Ellie shifted toward her grandmother. "Nana, want to eat with me?"

"I wouldn't miss it for the world."

Ellie tugged on her mom's arm and drew her toward the grill where Steve passed out the hot dogs. Her daughter's joy infected Julia, making it difficult to hold on to her annoyance at her mother. She'd almost sounded believable a few seconds ago. But Julia knew better. This morning she'd seen a softening, but when her mom returned to Chicago everything would return to the way it was.

"What did you think of the rodeo?" Evan asked in his Texan drawl when he came up behind her.

She shivered at his nearness.

"Cold?"

"No." She spun around to face him. "It's actually quite pleasant today. And I loved the mock rodeo, but more importantly, the children did."

"I'm not sure who had more fun, the kids or me."

He took a step toward her. She receded the same distance until her back encountered the corral fence. Then nothing but a few inches separated them. He bent his head toward her to whisper, "I liked seeing you laugh."

Her mouth went dry. She glimpsed the children and adults a couple of hundred yards away, busy loading their plates with lunch. The scent of dust, animal and leather accosted her, not unpleasantly. The gleam in Evan's eyes teased her, urging her to forget that over twenty people weren't far away.

"I like laughing," she finally managed to squeak out, realizing she'd done a lot of that in his company.

The rough tips of his fingers grazed across

her cheek and dug into her hair. "You aren't as tense as you were when you arrived. Are you and your mother getting along better?"

Breathless, she tried to think of an answer, but all her mind could focus on was him, so close she was sure that he could hear her heart pounding against her chest.

"Julia?" The corner of his mouth turned upward.

"What was your question?"

"How are you doing with your mom?"

"Actually, better than I thought." She had to look to the side of him, or she wouldn't have been able to answer. There was something elusive in his expression that drew her. She couldn't quite figure out what it was.

"What's different from last night? I got the impression you two would go to battle before the evening was over."

Her gaze met his. "We almost did. But I went to bed early and prayed. This morning Mom seemed more relaxed. I heard Ellie and her talking some as I was trying to sleep."

"That's good. Grandparents are special to a child. That's why I put up with Marge."

"The problem is I don't know if this is a one-shot deal. So she came this weekend, but what about in the future? I'm afraid this is like dangling a treat before Ellie's eyes."

"Then can you ask your mother what her plans are?"

Julia sucked in a deep breath. "I know I need to, but I'm even more afraid of what her answer will be."

"But once you know it, you'll be able to prepare Ellie."

"You're right. I just wish you weren't."

"Haven't you figured it out yet that I'm always right?"

"I've figured out you are cocky, arrogant and stubborn." She flattened her hands on his chest and gently pushed him away before she really did forget they weren't alone and did something she would regret, like kiss him. She had to keep reminding herself they were strictly friends.

She slipped past him as a car came down the road. Peddling backward, she said, "That's Sarah and Ali. I'm glad he's able to come for lunch. It's been a rough week for him with the general's death and then coming home from the hospital to a new house."

Evan strode toward her. "But you were able to get Sarah named his foster parent. That is good."

"Her living next door to the general does make the transition easier for Ali. As soon as he is well, he's going to start school and be in her kindergarten class."

"Then it's good that he gets to meet his classmates in a situation like this." Evan halted near Sarah's car and opened the passenger's door. He greeted Ali in Arabic, then said in English, "Welcome to the Double P Ranch."

The small child's dark gaze took in his surroundings. When it lit upon a horse, it brightened.

"After you eat, if it's okay, I'll take you to see the horses." Evan took the boy's hand and led him toward the tables and the other children who immediately swarmed around him, introducing themselves.

"This was a good idea, Julia." Sarah shut her car door. "He tries not to act sad around me, but I can see it in his eyes."

"It'll take time. This year has been so traumatic for him. He lost his mother and grandfather, on top of having to have heart surgery and moving to a new country."

"I know. But I want the best for him *now*."

"You sound like a mother."

"I'm already feeling like one."

"Good. He'll need your love to help him get

over all that he's gone through." Julia strolled toward the party that was in full swing.

Before her were so many snapshots for her to cherish—the children accepting Ali as one of their own, her daughter laughing with Paige, Evan talking to her mother, who had a huge smile on her face.

Then she thought of the conversation she needed to have with her mother, and she realized this was the calm before the storm.

Later that evening after her daughter fell into bed, exhausted but happy, Julia waited at the doorway for her mother to kiss Ellie good night.

In the short hallway Julia said, "Would you like me to fix some decaf?"

"That would be nice."

Julia made her way to the kitchen with her mother trailing behind her. After quickly preparing the coffee while her mom chattered about the wonderful birthday party Ellie had, Julia brought two mugs to the table and sat, sliding one toward her mother.

"We need to talk."

Chapter Seven

"**W**hat's there to talk about?" Julia's mom asked and blew on her coffee.

"Is this trip a one-time deal?" Julia studied her mother's expression for any hint of her motive for the sudden visit.

She carefully placed her mug on the wooden table. "I don't know."

"Well, at least you're being honest. So we shouldn't expect you to visit again anytime in the near future?"

Her mother flinched. "I guess I deserve that."

"I should have told you not to come."

"Why?"

"Because all you've managed to do was get my daughter's hopes up that she'll have a relationship with her grandmother, when in reality we're going to go back to the way it was—almost nonexistent."

"What do you want me to do? Go against your father?"

"Frankly, yes. Ellie shouldn't have to pay for my mistake." Hand trembling, Julia lifted her drink to her lips and sipped.

"I know, but I don't think he's going to change. I've tried talking to him about this."

"So you do agree with me? Then why aren't you more involved in Ellie's life?"

"Because I'm used to keeping the peace around the house." Her mother sighed.

"Isn't my daughter worth standing up to Dad for?" When her mother remained silent, just staring down at her coffee, Julia asked, "Why did you come now?"

"Your father went on his annual fishing trip, and I thought it would be a good time to come."

"He has gone every year since Ellie's birth. Why now, Mom?" Julia sensed something wasn't right—her mother's sudden averted gaze, her fingers tapping the tabletop, one of her nervous habits.

"Do I have to have a reason to want to see my granddaughter?"

"Yes, under the circumstances."

Her mom dropped her head and folded her hands in her lap. "Two months ago I was diagnosed with breast cancer. The doctor thinks he got it all, and I'm having radiation treatments so I'm not too worried."

Stunned, Julia straightened in her chair. "Why didn't you tell me?"

"It's behind me. Having cancer, though, has made me reconsider certain aspects in my life. One is that I want to know my only grandchild. Life is too short to let anger and pride rule it."

"Tell that to Dad."

"I have, but he won't listen. There's something he's not telling me. I know it, but I don't know what it is."

"Will you keep this visit from him?"

Her mother shook her head. "I can't lie to him. Besides, I want to tell him what a beautiful granddaughter he has. She's growing up into quite a nice young lady." Cradling the mug in both hands, she took a long drink of her coffee. "I intend to call Ellie more often and perhaps see her a couple of times a year if I can swing the price of an airplane ticket. We live on a budget since your father retired early last year."

Elation mingled with sadness. Julia was happy her mother would have a relationship with Ellie, but she wanted the same from her father. A tightness in her chest contracted when she thought of all the missed opportunities for Ellie and her dad. Her past pain wouldn't even allow her to address her own feelings involving not having a relationship with her parents. All she would let herself do is focus on her child.

"Honey, it's getting late and I have to leave early in the morning." Her mother rose.

"Stay awhile longer."

"I can't. I'll have to ease your father into this new situation. You know how he is about change." She reached out and clasped her arm. "But things will be different in the future."

Julia surged to her feet and went into her mom's embrace. Tears, held inside for so long, streaked down her cheeks. "I've missed you, Mom. So much."

When she pulled back, she smiled, though her own eyes held tears. "I want you to know I like Evan Paterson. He would make a great father for Ellie."

"Mom! We aren't dating." Heat flooded her face.

"You could have fooled me. Have you noticed how he looks at you? Snatch him up quickly before he gets away."

"You didn't say anything to him, did you?" Panic gripped her. She'd caught her mother and Evan talking on more than one occasion today.

"I might have mentioned once or twice what a good mother you are."

Although elated at her mother's compliment, Julia groaned, not sure if she could show her face to him anytime soon. How long would it take for him to forget his conversation with her mother?

The second Evan parked next to the church, Paige hopped out of the truck and raced toward the front lawn where they would set up the table to sell hot chocolate. Keeping an eye on his daughter as he followed, he realized he had an incoming call.

"Paterson here."

"Mr. Paterson, this is Nathan Staton with the *Dallas Sentinel*. Would you care to comment on this latest development on the disappearance of your sister? Do you think she was kidnapped?"

Evan stiffened. "I don't know what happened to Whitney. All I want is my sister returned home safely."

"What do you think of John's amnesia?"

"Nothing and I don't like your tone. Goodbye." Evan snapped the cell phone closed and stuffed it into his pocket.

His hands shook as he combed his fingers through his hair. His heartbeat thundered in his head. John and Whitney had been happily married and to hint otherwise angered Evan. Why the need to make more out of the story? Wasn't it tragic enough that his sister was still missing?

He couldn't control what others did, but he could control his reaction. He wasn't going to let that reporter dampen the day. Shoving the call from his mind, he headed toward Paige.

Evan saw Julia pull into the church parking lot, and the sight of her lifted his spirits. Her mother was right. She was a good parent. Any man would be lucky to have her as his wife.

"Paige!" Dressed in blue jeans and a red-and-white shirt, Ellie ran ahead of Julia. Both girls had decided to wear their hair pulled back in a ponytail with a red bow and white stars.

"It looks like they're ready to sell hot chocolate at the Veterans Day parade." Julia showed him the poster she carried. "This is for the front of the table."

"'Paige and Ellie's hot-chocolate stand, all proceeds go to the troops in the Middle East.'"

He pointed to several gold stars. "I like the glitter. That ought to attract some customers."

"Personally, I think it will be their smiles that do it, but Ellie did have fun decorating the poster."

"You sound like a mother." *Why couldn't Paige have a mother who cared?*

"That's because I am." Julia set her tote bag on the ground and began unloading it, passing a couple of American flags to Evan.

"How's the new pet doing?" he asked as he put one flag on each corner of the table.

"Let's see." She tapped her chin and looked skyward. "Besides the half bottle of glitter all over him and my apartment, Mr. Whiskers is settling right in. The best thing is he knows where the litter box is."

"That is nice."

She paused, eyeing him. "Did I hear mockery in your voice?"

He grinned. "No way! I have to spend the day with you." Then he winked. "Are y'all ready?"

"Yes, Daddy. We are gonna make big money for the soldiers."

"And they will be grateful for your package. It will get there in time for the holidays." He taped the poster to the front of the table. "We probably should have put some flyers up around downtown to let people know. At least I managed to get it in the Sunday paper."

Julia bent over her tote bag and whipped out a stack of papers. "While we were doing the poster last night, I decided to do a few flyers."

"Great minds think alike. Ellie, since you had a hand in these, do you want to go and put them up with your mom?"

Julia's daughter glanced at Paige, and he was positive something passed between them that he didn't want to know, but probably should.

"We'd rather stay here in case someone comes by early and wants some hot chocolate," his daughter said with such innocence on her face.

"Yeah, you and Mommy can do that." Ellie's expression mirrored Paige's.

"We can't leave you two alone." Julia withdrew a hammer and some nails. "Only one of us has to do it."

Paige leaned forward and waved toward someone behind Evan. "Hi, Reverend Fields. Daddy and Julia need to hang up flyers. Can you watch me and Ellie while they do?"

Evan turned toward the older man. "You don't have—"

"It will be my pleasure, and I want to be the

first customer for a cup." He plunked down a dollar bill.

"Thank you." Paige snatched it up and stuffed it in their money bag then zipped it close.

After placing the paper cup in front of her, Ellie stood and carefully filled it all the way to the top. When she handed it to the reverend, she sloshed a little on her hand and the tablecloth. A frown formed on her mouth.

"I guess I'd better not pour so much." Ellie watched Reverend Fields as he took his first sip. "Is it okay? Mommy made it."

"Perfect. This is delicious, Julia. I'm going to have you make it for our church events from now on." He motioned with his hands. "You two go on and get those flyers up. People should have a cup of this. I hope you have made a lot."

"I bought some extra ingredients if I have to make some more. I was hoping you would let us use the church kitchen."

"I insist on it. This is for a good cause. And I have an extra hammer. Let me go get it." The reverend hurried toward the building.

"If you give me the keys, I'll get the supplies and put them in the kitchen. Three large thermoses won't last thirty minutes into the parade. Besides, afterward people tend to mill around downtown." Taking Julia's keys, Evan jogged toward her car.

He carried the box into the church, peering around for the reverend. When he saw him backing out of a closet in the hallway that led to the kitchen, he headed toward him.

"Franklin, I'm sticking this box in the kitchen. Can you wait a sec?" He quickly set the extra supplies on the counter just inside the door, then hastened back to the reverend.

"How are things going for you, Evan?"

"That's what I want to talk to you about. I know this isn't the best time. If I don't get back outside soon, I'll have a little girl hunting for me. But can we talk later? Tomorrow? The next day?"

"How about at two tomorrow?"

"That would be great. Then I can pick up Paige from school. She always likes that. She's been complaining the bus ride is too long." Evan strolled from the church with the reverend next to him.

"I imagine Paige is one of the last ones let off."

"Yeah. This time of year I'm not as busy, so I make it a habit of picking her up a couple of times a week. That usually keeps her quiet, but when spring comes, I won't have any time."

The reverend stopped about ten yards away from the two girls and Julia. "Is that what you want to talk about, Paige?"

"No." He glanced toward Julia. "I had everything planned out and now I don't know what to do."

"Ah, I see." The older man peered at Julia, too. He patted Evan on the back. "We'll talk tomorrow. Go hang up the flyers and enjoy today. I'll watch the girls until you two get back."

Julia had covered her side of the street and finished putting up her last flyer. Spying Evan by the hardware store, she jogged across the four lanes toward him. The police had blocked off the parade route and people were beginning to congregate on the sidewalk.

"This is a big deal. Since this was a weekday, I didn't think there would be a large crowd." Julia looked up and down Veterans Boulevard.

"A lot of offices shut down a little early so everyone can attend and show their support for the troops. Prairie Springs depends on Fort Bonnell."

"So, in the long run it's good business to close early."

"I'm sure that motivates some, but this is an army town."

"I noticed some signs up in the stores that they would reopen after the parade."

"While the people are in town, they will shop, so naturally they will reopen. Now that's good business."

Julia laughed. "Everyone scratches each others' back. I like that."

"That's the way a society should operate. Mutual respect." Evan pounded his nail into the pole, putting up the last flyer. "Done. I had a few people ask me about the hot chocolate."

"So did I." Julia started back toward the church across from the town green at midpoint on Veterans Boulevard. "I hope the girls do well. I told Ellie I would take her and Paige shopping for the items for the troops."

"Will you let an old soldier tag along with y'all?"

"Sure. How about Friday? After we get the gifts, we can go back to my apartment, have something to eat and pack the supplies up."

"Then I can mail them the next day."

"We're a good team," Julia said. Her last thought was out loud and immediately she wished she could take back the words, not because they weren't true, but because of the look on his face.

Evan stopped in the middle of the busy sidewalk with people passing them on both sides and stared long and hard into her eyes. Soon after the crowd around them became part of the background. She knew they were there, but they didn't matter.

Every one of her senses seemed to be focused solely on Evan. His aftershave in the crispy air. The feel of his fingers around hers, his skin in stark contrast to her softer hands roughened by his work on the ranch. His eyes, totally on her.

Someone jostled into her and pushed her closer to him. He steadied her and began walking again, his arm around her as though it was important to keep her near. Contentment cocooned her.

"We'd better head back. I want to make sure that Ellie puts on her heavier coat." Although it would be nice to take a leisurely stroll with Evan and enjoy the fragrance of the crisp fall air, Julia quickened her pace, starting to feel the cooler temperature of the oncoming evening.

As she approached the church, she distanced herself from Evan a little. Aware of Ellie and Paige's conspiratorial whisperings when they got together, she didn't want the girls to get the wrong idea. That would be all she needed—for their daughters to be further encouraged to try and get them together as a couple. Olga was bad enough.

The reverend stood directly behind Ellie and Paige, keeping an eye on the girls and the line of people while one person after another bought a cup of hot chocolate. The smiles on the girls' faces attested to their success.

"This is wonderful," an old lady said as she passed Julia and Evan on the sidewalk. "I may even have a second cup."

Julia locked gazes with Evan. She said, "I need to make more," at the same time he said, "You need to make more."

When Julia arrived at the table, Ellie emptied the second container of hot chocolate and gave the cup to a distinguished gentleman in the front of the small line that had formed. Julia gathered up both thermoses to take with her into the church.

As the first strains of a march boomed through the air, Olga scurried toward them. "Everyone's talking about the hot chocolate. What a wonderful way to raise money for the troops! Has anyone seen my daughter? She said she was going to watch the parade from here."

"She and David went into the church. They should be back soon." The reverend shifted from one foot to the other, his intent gaze fastened on Olga as though he hadn't seen her in a while.

Julia needed to make more hot chocolate, but she hated to leave. Sparks flew between Franklin and Olga—a person would have to be blind not to see them. But it was just as obvious the reverend wasn't interested romantically in Olga. Others had commented to her they didn't understand why he wasn't. They were both single, involved in the church and shared a lot of the same interests. But she understood why. Loving someone was a risk he wasn't prepared to take—just like her.

Instead of going into the church to search for her daughter, Olga positioned herself next to Franklin. "The youth group's float is toward the end of the parade. I was down at the start, helping to put the finishing touches on it."

"I'd better get the hot chocolate made," Julia said when she saw more people standing in line.

"Do you need any help?" the reverend asked.

"Sure." Any second Julia expected to see the older man run his finger under his collar.

Together she and Franklin strolled toward the building, the reverend taking one thermos from her grasp.

Margaret Daley   159

"Thanks for the help."

"I should be the one thanking you." Franklin opened the door to the church and let her go inside first.

"I figured you needed rescuing."

"Am I that obvious?"

"Yep, afraid so."

"Olga is a special woman who has given so much to the congregation."

"But?" Julia placed her thermos on the counter in the kitchen and began mixing some ingredients for the drink. "You can stir this while the chocolate is melting."

Situating himself in front of the stove, the reverend clasped a wooden spoon. "I'm not ready to move on."

"When do you know you are ready?" Julia measured the milk.

"Well…" He continued to slowly blend the melting chocolate with the sugar and spices. He shot her a glance. "I guess you just know when you are."

In the short time she'd known the reverend, he usually had a ready answer, but the hesitation that sounded in his voice accentuated his doubts. "Do you think you hold on to the familiar because change is so scary?"

"That's a possibility." Another look slid her way. "Are we talking about you and Evan?"

She shrugged. Confusion reigned in her mind and heart.

"Change is a part of life."

"I know." Julia added the liquid to the pan on the stove. "I care for Evan. Goodness, my daughter certainly would like to see us together. Actually both of our daughters would, but I can't do it just for Ellie."

"No, you have to do it for yourself."

"What if I can't separate the two? I don't want to get involved for the wrong reasons."

"Then I suggest you pray about it." Franklin stepped to the side to give her room to tend to her pan on the stove. "What happened to make you so leery of a commitment?"

For a long moment Julia watched the melting chocolate swirl in the sugary substance, then she began telling the reverend about Clayton and her parents. He was the second person she had shared her story with in a short time, and as the words spilled out she felt a burden lift from her shoulders.

"I know I'm going to state the obvious, but not all men are like Clayton." The reverend poured the first pan's liquid into the tall thermos. "You say the Lord has forgiven you for your mistake, but have you forgiven yourself? I hear something in your voice, especially when you're talking about your parents, that makes me wonder if you have."

"I love my daughter with all my heart."

"But have you come to terms with your guilt?"

Had she? Although she and her mother had improved their relationship since her visit, she still felt guilty for her impulsive action seven years ago. She'd allowed herself to surrender to the moment and be talked into something she had known in her heart wasn't right—at least not for her.

"Come in, Evan." Franklin gestured toward the couch in his office. "Have a seat. How did the fund-raiser turn out?"

"We raised over two hundred dollars. A lot of people gave more than the girls charged for the drink. The town has always been so generous toward the soldiers." Evan folded his length onto the couch, shifting toward the reverend who was in a lounge chair nearby.

"That's one of the reasons I was drawn to Prairie Springs. The town and base blend so effortlessly." He crossed his legs and put a pad he held on the end table next to him. "So, tell me why you wanted to see me."

"This won't come as a surprise with all the time Julia and I have spent together, but I'm finding myself interested in her against my better judgment."

"Why do you say that?"

"You're aware of my wife's death at the beginning of the year."

"I officiated over her funeral."

"Yes. Yes, of course, you did." Evan inhaled several gulps of air, not sure how to explain the conflicting emotions swirling around inside him. "Have you ever been drawn to something that you know isn't good for you?"

Franklin's eyebrows rose. "You don't think Julia's good for you?"

"Don't get me wrong. Julia is a wonderful woman and would make a great mother for Paige, but is that enough to base a relationship on?"

"No. So you're telling me there couldn't be more between you and Julia?"

Evan glanced away, realizing he hadn't really expressed his feelings well. "No, on the contrary, I think there could be something between us if I let myself."

"Then what's stopping you?"

"Diane."

"Are you still in love with your deceased wife?"

"No!" Frustrated at his inability to get his point across, he blew a breath out between pursed lips. "I *know* I'm not, haven't been for a long time. My marriage to Diane, even before I left for the Middle East, wasn't a strong one. I realize that now. I shouldn't have been so stunned when she left me, but I was. It rocked my world and left me…" He searched for the right word. "Unsure of my ability to know what is best for me."

"So rather than take a chance on seeing where a relationship with Julia would lead, you would rather be alone?"

Evan nodded, his stomach churning.

The reverend leaned forward, resting his elbows on the arms of his chair and steepling his fingers together. "I haven't told anyone this, but five years ago after my wife and son were killed in a car accident the day before Connor was to report to Fort Bonnell for basic training, I decided I'd had a great relationship with my wife and that was my one allotment."

"Exactly."

"But by your own words your marriage wasn't a good one." Franklin grinned. "And actually that isn't even the point. There is no certain amount of happiness a person gets. I'm starting to see that now. Don't end up lonely like me."

"Then date Olga."

"I could say the same thing to you. Date Julia, see where it will lead you two."

"I don't want Paige to end up hurt in all of this. She's lost one mother. I wouldn't want her to become attached to Julia and lose her, too."

"Are we talking about Paige or you?"

Surprise trembled through him. "To be honest, both."

"Life's a risk. We can only control a fraction of it. We have a say over what choices we make and how we respond to what happens to us. You have a choice and yes, you, and even Paige, could get hurt by that choice, but you could also make the best decision for yourself by grabbing this opportunity."

Evan rolled to his feet. "You've given me a lot to think about." He slid his hand into his pocket for his truck keys. "I'm not sure what I decide will make any difference in the long run. Julia is equally as leery of a romantic relationship."

"That may be true. You can't control her. You can only control your actions, but if you don't try, you'll never know." The reverend rose and walked Evan to the side entrance of the church. "Pray to the Lord for guidance."

"What if He doesn't hear my prayer?"

"He always hears our prayers. We may not always get the answer we're looking for, however."

"How about you and Olga?" Evan pushed open the door.

"I need more time. Perhaps one day."

Chapter Eight

Evan tore off his plaid shirt and tossed it on the bed. He looked like he was going out to the barn to work, not shopping with Julia and the girls. Facing his open closet, he scanned his few choices. He realized he should have done some laundry. Maybe even shopped for new clothes for himself.

He yanked a long-sleeved beige turtleneck from its hanger. He stuffed his arms into it, pulled it over his head and tucked it into his black jeans. He refused to look at himself in the mirror because he had nothing else to wear.

And why in the world was he obsessing about it anyway?

Because I'm nervous.

Sinking down on his bed, he pulled on his

black boots. He hadn't felt this way in years, and he didn't like it.

He was going to ask Julia on a date tonight. The reverend's words had wormed their way into his mind, and he couldn't rid himself of the image of being old, by himself, in an empty house with Paige living her own life.

It's just a date. You aren't going to ask her to marry you.

Yeah, he could do this.

"Daddy, we're gonna be late. C'mon."

"Coming." He snatched up the keys off his dresser and headed out the door.

"Mommy, they're gonna be here any minute. Hurry up." Ellie stood in the entrance to Julia's bedroom.

With her brush poised next to her head, Julia studied herself in the mirror. Her hair simply wouldn't cooperate. Her usual waves were frizzy. Why did it have to rain that day?

"You look beautiful." Her hands on her hips, Ellie came inside a few feet.

"Did you set the table?"

"Yes."

Julia inhaled a deep breath, catching the scent of the beef stew she had in the Crock-Pot. After running the brush one final time through her hair, she gathered it up and snapped in a large mother-of-pearl clip to hold her wayward tresses at her nape.

"Okay. I'm ready."

The doorbell chimed.

Ellie whirled around and raced from the room. "I'll get it."

"Be sure to check to see…" Her words trailed off as she faced an empty space where her daughter had been only seconds before.

Grabbing her purse with the kids' money, Julia followed her daughter into the living room. When Ellie opened the door, Paige flew into the apartment, but Evan stood framed in the entrance, his large presence dominating the space.

The sight of him stole her breath. Rugged. Handsome. Fatherly. A nice combination.

"Are y'all ready to go spend some money?" he said with a gleam in his eyes as he rubbed his hands together.

"Yes," both girls shouted and jumped in the air.

"Mmm. Dinner smells great! What is it?" Evan stepped to the side to allow Paige and Ellie to barrel out into the hallway.

"Beef stew. I'll put the bread in when we get back here. And if you all are good—" she fixed her gaze on first Ellie then Paige "—we'll have a French silk pie I made."

"Mommy makes the best pies."

"Chocolate. Be still my heart." Evan splayed his hand over his chest.

Julia headed down the hall, the kids skipping ahead of her. "I thought you might like that."

"Do I have to be good, too?"

"Especially you. If not, the girls and I will be sharing the whole pie."

"Oh, you're cruel, Julia Saunders. You know how much I love chocolate."

"Yes, I do. I had to do something to keep you in line."

Outside, Paige and Ellie ran to the truck and hopped into the backseat. The sun had disappeared on the horizon as night settled in. The brisk wind chilled Julia. She shivered and quickened her pace.

"I can't believe Thanksgiving is next week. Before long Christmas will be here." Julia climbed into the cab, and Evan shut her door and rounded the front of his vehicle.

"Do you think it will snow this year?" Ellie asked.

"It hardly ever snows here," Paige said and put her seat belt on.

Evan started his truck. "It's feeling pretty cold right now. I should have gotten out our heavy coats."

"Could it snow tonight?"

The excitement in her daughter's voice reminded Julia of last winter when they had made a huge snowman on the apartment lawn in Chicago. "The rain has moved out of the area so even if it gets cold enough it won't snow."

"Where are we going?"

"The Super Center. It should have everything we need," Evan answered his daughter.

Paige leaned forward. "After we shop, can we look at the toys?"

"Fine." Evan drove into the massive parking lot and pulled up to the main doors. "Y'all get out, and I'll find a parking space. No sense in all of us freezing."

The girls ran ahead of Julia into the store. Wind blew trash and leaves across her path to the entrance. She hugged her sweater to her and hurried her pace.

Inside, Paige and Ellie already had the shopping cart. They danced about it as if they'd had too much sugar. Julia would need to cut their piece of the pie in half if they didn't settle down soon.

"Ready?" Evan asked as he came up behind Julia, his hand brushing across the small of her back.

"The girls have a list of supplies the soldiers might need." Julia retrieved it from her purse and scanned it. "Let's start with the toiletry items."

Paige headed for the section with Ellie right behind her. Evan pushed the cart at a slower pace.

"Aren't you worried that they might be pulling everything off the shelves at this very moment?"

"I probably should be, but while they aren't here, I thought I would see if you would like to go out to dinner tomorrow night with me."

"Dinner?" Her voice squeaked at the unexpected invitation.

"If you've got plans, I understand. I shouldn't—"

"I'd love to go with you. What time?"

"You would?"

It was his turn for his voice to sound funny. Julia pressed her lips together to keep her chuckle from escaping. They certainly were a pair!

"Yes, if I can get my neighbor to babysit for me. I'll check when we get back to the apartment."

"C'mon, y'all. What's takin' y'all so long?" Paige stood at the end of an aisle with one hand on her hip, tapping her foot.

When Julia turned into the aisle, she halted, her gaze on her daughter in the middle.

Evan bumped into her with the cart. "Sorry. What's the—" He peered toward the girls.

Ellie's arms were full of tubes of toothpaste, every brand on the shelf, which would soon be empty at the rate Paige was scooping up the rest.

Evan worked his mouth, but no words came out.

"Eleanor Rose, put every tube back in its correct place. Now!"

"But we need toothpaste. That's on our list."

Several deep breaths later, Julia said, "If we're going to buy a variety of products, then we'll need to limit the number of each item." She covered the distance to her daughter and plucked ten tubes from the stack in her arms. "We'll take these. Put the rest back."

"You, too, Paige. And from now on no running ahead of us." Evan leaned close to Julia's ear. "I wonder what it's gonna be like tomorrow night on our date without two little girls causing mischief."

Date! The implication of what she had agreed to struck her full force. She was going on a date, the first in years. What if she forgot how to act on one? Panic began to set in.

* * *

"That's the last box." Julia smoothed the packing tape across its top. "We're done. Five big packages for the troops."

Ellie clapped, and Paige pumped her arm into the air.

"Y'all did good. I'm proud of both of you for thinking to do something for the soldiers." Lifting the last box, Evan stacked it with the other four by the front door.

After Paige whispered something into Ellie's ear, her daughter leaped to her feet. "I want to show Paige my room. Can she stay for a while? Pleeeze."

"Fine, if it's okay with your mom."

Julia nodded.

"They're at it again," Evan said in a low voice as the two girls raced from the living room.

"You think? It's kinda interesting to see what they'll do next."

"They're probably plotting something as we speak."

Julia faced Evan. "So what do we do in the meantime?"

"Hmm, let me think." Rubbing his hand along his jaw, he stared at the ceiling. "Hey, I've got a novel idea. Let's sit, relax and do nothing."

"People do that?" she said with as serious a face as she could muster.

"I've heard of it." Evan walked to the couch and tested the softness of the cushion. "Nice. Comfortable. Want to try it with me?" Settling on the sofa, he patted the place next to him.

Julia didn't move. Eyeing him, she tried to decide if it was wise to sit so close to him.

He winked at her. "I promise I won't bite. I'm all bark."

She wiped her hand across her forehead. "Well, that's a relief. I was worried."

When she eased down beside him, she made sure there were several inches between them. She could hear her heart pounding. Did he?

A minute into the silence he chuckled. "This is a first for us."

Us! That sounded like they were a couple. "What do you mean?"

"At a loss for words." He shifted so he faced her on the couch, his arm resting on its back. "Did I surprise you when I asked you to dinner tomorrow night without the girls?"

"Yes. Why did you?" She was sure that question wasn't in any handbook on dating. A woman shouldn't expect a man to explain why he asked her on a date.

"Because I decided it was time we stop avoiding what we are feeling. I'm attracted to you, and when that occurs, a man usually asks the woman to go out with him."

"Oh." What should she say to that?

"Now you're at a loss for words."

"Only because you keep doing things I'm not expecting."

"What are you expecting?"

That was an excellent question, and she didn't have an answer for it. Four weeks ago she could have. Not now. "We're friends," she said because he was waiting for a reply.

"And friends can never start dating?"

"Why have you changed your mind?"

"Because I'm fighting myself on this one. Just like you, I don't want to get hurt again, but frankly it's getting hard to be around you and not want to get to know you better." He shrugged. "What can I say? I'm an all-or-nothing kind of guy."

"Okay, so we try dating and see where it leads us. If nowhere, do we go our separate ways?"

Evan stared at a place on the wall across the room. When he peered at her, a neutral expression fell over his features. "Probably would be the wisest thing. I never want my daughter to be hurt, and if we continued to be around each other, both of them would try to get us together."

"Because Ellie wants a father and Paige, a mother."

"Yep, but I know I would never marry just to give my daughter a mother. One bad experience was enough for me." He took both of Julia's hands, tugging her closer to him. "But I am willing to see if our daughters are right. Do we belong together?"

Another excellent question. Again she had no answer. She drew in a composing breath before releasing it slowly. "I think you're right. We should see where our growing friendship leads. I care about you and Paige." A lot, she added silently, but not willing to go that far yet.

His eyelids slid halfway down, but that didn't take away from the power behind his look. It pierced through the armor around her heart and penetrated clear through. He closed the short distance between them, moving his hands up her arms to embrace her. When she tilted her head back slightly, his lips were on hers, and she surrendered to the reeling sensations spiraling through her.

When he pulled back a few inches, she didn't

want to let him go. His kiss had rocked her world. For a brief moment visions of not being alone, having someone to share her joy and her sorrow, played across her mind.

She straightened, breaking totally away. The pictures were too tempting. Shoring up her defenses, she rose on shaky legs.

"I need to check on the girls. They're being awfully quiet. That's when a parent has to worry the most." She didn't care that she was chattering or that Evan gave her a puzzled look. She had to put some space between them—preferably several rooms for now.

She made her way to Ellie's bedroom. As she approached it, she heard her daughter say, "Yeah, I like that. It's always just me and Mommy."

Julia stepped into the doorway with a smile on her face although she couldn't stop wondering what the two were plotting.

"Mommy, Paige asked us to Thanksgiving dinner next week. It's gonna be just her and her daddy because her grandma is going to her sister's house. Can we?"

Although Evan was quiet in his movement, Julia didn't have to glance down the hall to know that he was coming. "Paige, I think that's something your dad has to decide."

"Decide what?" Evan stopped in the entrance next to Julia.

Attuned to his presence, she had a hard time remaining focused on the girls and the answer to his question. "Paige wants us to have Thanksgiving dinner with you."

"I hadn't thought about Thanksgiving."

Paige stood, her arms stiff at her sides. "We never have Thanksgiving dinner at our house. Can't we this year? You're learning to cook. Please, Daddy."

"I'll bring the dessert and anything else you need, if that will help."

"French silk pie?" His eyes gleamed. "That was delicious tonight."

"Are you sure you don't want the traditional pies—pumpkin and pecan?"

"Yep, one hundred percent sure. French silk will be just fine."

"Anything else you need in the way of food?"

"Hmm." Evan scratched his head. "Nope. But don't be surprised if this dinner isn't exactly the traditional meal y'all are used to. But I figure a turkey can't be too hard to fix. Just stick it in the oven and turn it on to the temperature it says." His breath brushed across her ear as he whispered, "My teacher has taught me the importance of reading directions. So I think I can do this."

"Then we are going?" Ellie positioned herself next to Paige as though they were a united front.

Julia swung her attention to her daughter. "Yes."

The two girls cheered as if their team had scored a touchdown, which only worried Julia.

"Are you warm enough?" Seated on the park bench, a streetlight casting a glow on it, Evan settled his arm around Julia's shoulder and drew her against his side.

"Yes. It's not as cold as it was last night and there's no wind. I enjoyed the dinner at Bette's Bar-b-que and Ribs. I'd heard good things about the steaks and every one of them was right."

Evan checked his watch. "We've got a while before the movie starts, but we don't have to sit out here."

"No, it's nice."

Although in the middle of downtown, the large town green gave them the feeling of isolation from the rest of the world. Across the street people walked along the sidewalk, coming and going from the restaurants and the few stores that remained open. Even on this main thoroughfare there were several large Victorian structures that reflected the quaintness that she had come to love about Prairie Springs.

"Have you ever wondered what it was like here a hundred years ago?" Julia asked and snuggled closer to him.

"Sometimes when I'm out tending my cattle on my ranch, I can easily picture myself living in the late 1800s doing the very same thing."

"Did you always want to be a rancher?"

"Are you kidding? I grew up in Texas. I'm sure half the male population at one time or another wanted to be a cowboy."

"Then why did you go into the army?"

He looked skyward. "When I first went into the army, I couldn't imagine bringing a child into this world unless it was safer. I always wanted to be a father. So I decided I had to do something about making the world safer."

"Too bad not everyone feels that way."

"In a perfect world they would."

"In the one to come."

"I learned about Jesus in the army from the chaplain at the base I was at after basic training. I can't imagine what combat would have been like without Christ in my life." Tension gripped him. "Why isn't He answering my prayers about Whitney?"

She angled toward him, grasping his hand in hers. "Be patient. He will answer you."

"She's been missing in action for *months*. How much more patient do I have to be? I think not knowing what happened is the worst." Anguish riddled his voice.

"So the raid in the north, where they had heard rumors of a couple being held hostage, wasn't true?"

"No, the place was empty. If she had been there, she was gone by the time our guys arrived." His fingers clasped hers tighter. "I've been a good Christian, doing what the Lord wanted. What do I have to do to get my sister back?"

"Turn it over to the Lord. You aren't in control of the situation. Let Him handle it."

"I'm not good at turning control over to anyone. Two years ago my life changed drastically. Being organized and maintaining control over certain situations have been what has kept me sane." He threw her a wry grin. "That's one of the reasons I'm my own boss."

"But do you have total control over the ranch? What happens if the weather turns bad or a disease sweeps through your herd?"

"I'll deal with it. I know unexpected things happen, but the day-to-day operation works well because of what I put in place."

"The point is, unexpected things will always happen in life. You can be going along just fine and suddenly you are slammed with a huge problem that alters the direction of your life."

His arm slid from her shoulder, and he took her other hand. "Are we talking about me, or what happened to you when you became pregnant with Ellie?"

"Both. I had everything mapped out for myself. I was going to finish school. Clayton and I were going to get married and then start a family maybe two or three years later. I felt like a Mack truck had run me over."

"I know the feeling, and it wasn't easy scraping myself off the ground." One corner of his mouth hitched upward.

Drawn by his half smile, Julia leaned into him. He inched closer.

"We need to go if we're gonna see the movie," he murmured against her mouth.

"What movie?" All common sense fled as she leaned into him, his arms bracketed around her.

His chuckles tickled her lips. "The one you wanted to see."

"Oh, that one."

The brush of his mouth across hers drove away all thoughts about the movie. Her pulse increased. The real world faded.

Until Evan's cell phone blared and he jerked back. He fished for it and answered the call.

She was falling in love. That thought should panic her. Surprisingly, it didn't.

Her mind in a daze, Julia didn't listen to his conversation at first, but an urgency in his voice penetrated her fog, pulling her back to the here and now.

"Yes, Marge, I'll be right there. That's okay. I just finished dinner." He snapped his cell phone closed and stuffed it into his pant pocket.

"What's wrong?"

"Paige found Diane's journal that Marge had from her daughter's belongings. I didn't even know about it."

"Paige read it?"

"No, but she recognized her mother's name and asked Marge about it. Paige wanted her grandmother to read it to her. She said she couldn't because I didn't want her to have it. My daughter ran into the bathroom and locked herself in. Marge says she is wailing."

"I thought you didn't know about it."

"I didn't, but I told Marge I didn't want any of Diane's belongings, that she could keep them for Paige when she was older." Evan rose. "I need to go talk to her."

"Do you want me to come with you?"

"Would you? This isn't something I have much experience dealing with."

"If I can help, I will." Julia fell into step beside Evan back to his truck pulled next to the restaurant.

Ten minutes later they were parked in the driveway of a ranch-style home a few blocks from the downtown area. Evan stared at the house ablaze with lights. He didn't move.

"I've been thinking. I wonder how Paige found the journal," Evan said, drumming his fingers on the steering wheel.

"Do you think your mother-in-law had it where your daughter would find it?"

"That's definitely a possibility. After Diane died, she wanted to give everything of Diane's that she brought back from California to Paige. Paige was having a hard enough time coping. I didn't want her to have to deal with anything else."

"Did Marge tell you she had a journal?"

Opening the door, Evan slid her a sheepish

look. "No, but then I didn't give her much of a chance. I had my own problems dealing with Diane's desertion, let alone her death."

Julia climbed from the truck and followed him up to the front porch. The door opened even before he rang the bell. Her mouth set in a scowl, Marge blocked the entrance, her gaze sweeping toward Julia for a long moment. The urge to squirm engulfed her.

"Did I catch you at a bad time?" Marge directed the question at Evan.

"I told you I'd just finished eating dinner. Julia and I had a date this evening."

One of Marge's delicate eyebrows arched. "Y'all did? I'm so sorry to interrupt your 'date.' If you want I can take care of Paige. Y'all can continue your 'date' as if nothing is wrong."

"Marge, I'm here. I'd like to talk to my daughter now." Exasperation laced Evan's voice.

"Sure, if you think you have time for her." The older woman pivoted and marched into her living room off to the side of the entryway.

Evan rolled his eyes. "Sorry about this," he whispered and indicated for Julia to go first into the house.

"Don't worry about me. Go see Paige."

Evan headed toward the back of the house

while Julia entered the living room. Marge sat on the couch with the journal in her lap, her finger tracing around its edge. Still standing, Julia inspected her surroundings. Lots of framed photos, mostly of a young woman, spanned the length of the mantel. Stuffed pillows adorned the couch and two thick cushioned chairs with accompanying ottomans. Soft lighting cast a golden glow. A cozy feel lent a warmth and welcoming atmosphere to the house. She imagined Marge was a wonderful hostess and enjoyed entertaining.

In spite of what her daughter had done to Evan and Paige, Marge had still cared and accepted her, flaws and all. Julia wished she had that with her own parents.

His forehead furrowed, Evan came into the room and stopped next to Julia. Marge glanced up, a question in her gaze.

"Paige wouldn't open the door. Do you have a key for it?"

"No, I lost it years ago." Marge put the journal to the side of her. "I suppose we could call a locksmith."

"Let me try and talk to her first." Julia tensed as both Marge and Evan swerved their attention to her. "What do you have to lose?"

"Nothing. Please try," Evan said immediately before Marge spoke.

"Which way?"

"I'll show you." Evan steered her from the living room with a hand at the small of her back.

The scorn of the older woman's gaze burned a hole into her as she left. The sooner she got Paige out of the bathroom, the sooner she could leave.

Evan pointed to the only door in the long hallway that was closed. "Diane was Marge's whole life. She was devastated when her daughter left."

"I understand."

"I don't think she likes change any more than I do. I'll be in the living room, trying to repair the damage with her."

Julia rapped her knuckles against the door. "Paige, it's Julia. Can I talk to you?"

Silence.

"Is anyone else out there?"

"No, honey."

The shuffling of footsteps across tile sounded, then the lock clicked and the door inched open. Paige's pout filled the crack. "I don't wanna talk to anyone else."

"It's just me."

"Come in." Her eyes red, her cheeks streaked

with tears, Paige threw the door wide open and backed away.

Julia closed them in. Seeing the child so miserable tore at her heart. So much like her daughter, she wanted to hold the little girl close to her and wipe away any evidence of unhappiness.

Eyes shimmering, Paige stared at the tile floor for a few seconds, then lifted her head and looked right at her. Her bottom lip trembled. A tear coursed down her cheek.

Julia opened her arms wide, and Paige rushed into them. She closed them about the child and held her tightly. Her cries dampened the front of Julia's shirt as a lump formed in her throat.

"I miss Mommy so much."

"Of course you do, honey."

"Daddy is mad at Mommy." Paige raised her head and peered at her. "He doesn't like to talk about her."

"But you want to?"

She nodded. "I've tried with Grandma, but she starts crying."

"You can talk to me. I'm a good listener."

"Ellie thinks you're the best mommy."

A blush warmed Julia's cheeks.

Paige crunched her face into a deep frown. "Am I the reason Mommy went away?"

Chapter Nine

"Oh, honey, no. You're such a special little girl. Anybody would be blessed to have you as a daughter." Julia smoothed the child's hair away from her face, then cupped it, staring deep into her red swollen eyes. "Don't ever forget that."

Paige sniffed. "I won't."

"Why don't you tell me about your mother?"

"You want to know?" Paige's expression brightened.

"Yes, I want to know about the woman who had you." Julia sank down onto the lip of the tub, patting the porcelain area next to her.

"Mommy always smelled so good…"

"Marge, I'm going to move on with my life whether you like it or not. It would be easier for

Paige's sake if you accept that." Evan folded his arms across his chest and lounged back against the mantel.

His mother-in-law hugged her daughter's journal to her. "I know."

"Do you really?"

"Yes!" Marge stabbed him with a narrowed gaze. "You are making it abundantly clear you didn't love Diane."

"I did once. But I'm not the one who left."

"Yes, you did. You were gone for a year in the Middle East."

"I was serving my country. I was doing my job."

"Away from home. Away from Diane."

"She knew I was a soldier when we married."

Tears glistened in Marge's eyes. "I don't want Paige to forget her mother. Diane loved her."

"She had a funny way of showing it." The second he said that he regretted it.

A crestfallen expression drove the antagonism from Marge. "She was confused. She didn't know what she really wanted."

"Was that what she was doing in California?" Surprised by his surge of anger, Evan straightened, dropping his arms to his sides.

"I don't know what she was doing. I rarely

could get in touch with her." Tears fell from her eyes.

All frustration vanished. He could see his mother-in-law hurt as much as he did from Diane's leaving. Closing the space between them, he sat beside her on the couch.

"I didn't mean for Paige to see the journal. I was saving it for when she was older. I didn't realize she was going through that box in the closet."

"I wish you had let me know about the journal."

"You were so upset with Diane. I thought you would throw it away. Remember you told me to keep what I thought Paige might want someday."

When he had first heard about Diane's death, he was furious with her for wasting her life, turning to drugs for answers. She'd had a family who needed her, and she had walked away.

"Did you read it?" He stared at the hot-pink book in his mother-in-law's grasp.

Marge swiped the tears from her cheeks and faced him. "Yes, and Paige should know how her mother felt about her. She loved her daughter." She tapped the journal. "It's all in here."

"Then why did she leave her?"

"That's in here, too." She handed it to him.

"I guess I have some reading to do tonight. I want to go through it before I share it with Paige. I can't change what Diane did, but I can shield my daughter from being hurt any more than she already is."

Marge placed her hand over his on the book. "You won't regret sharing it with her."

"Daddy?"

He swiveled around to see Paige standing just inside the doorway with Julia next to her. Words refused to materialize in his mind.

"Why didn't you tell me about the diary?"

"Because he didn't know I had it," Marge said, drawing his daughter's attention to her.

"Then why didn't you?"

"I was going to when you were older," his mother-in-law said simply.

"I'm not a baby anymore." Paige clenched her hands to her sides.

"No, you aren't." Evan rose, gripping the journal. "And I'm going to share it with you after I read it tonight. Is that okay?"

Paige didn't say anything for a moment. Julia clasped his daughter's shoulder. Paige nodded.

"Please don't be angry with me, Paige." Marge pushed her heavy frame up so she stood next to Evan. "I didn't mean to hurt you."

"I know, Grandma. I'm not mad anymore. Julia helped me."

"Thank you for talking to Paige," his mother-in-law said and approached Julia holding out her hand.

Julia took it and shook it. "You're welcome. Paige is very special."

"I know." Marge turned to Evan's daughter. "Will you still spend the night?"

"Yes, Uncle Bert is supposed to teach me checkers when he gets home." A solemn expression filled his daughter's eyes as she skirted her grandmother and came to him. "Daddy, is that okay?"

"Yes, princess. We'll talk tomorrow after church about your mother's journal."

"Promise?"

"Yes, and you know I never break a promise." Evan tousled her hair, then dragged her to him to embrace her. "I love you."

"I love you, too, Daddy." She stepped back and threw a glance over her shoulder at Julia, then leaned close to whisper, "You can leave now. I'm okay. You could take Julia for an ice-cream cone. I know she likes them."

He laughed and winked. "I'll think of something."

Taking his hand, Paige hurried him toward the entry hall, peering back to make sure Julia was following. "Y'all have fun."

The closing of the front door teased a chuckle from him. "She finally realized she had interrupted our date."

"I had a wonderful time tonight."

"You did?"

"Yes," Julia said and ambled toward his truck. "I got to know you and your daughter better."

"I'm glad you were there. No telling how long I would have been pounding on that bathroom door." He helped her up into the cab.

"I'm sure she would have taken pity on you in an hour or so."

He strode to the driver's side and climbed in. "Whatever you said to her was perfect. I'm in your debt."

"I didn't really say a lot. I mostly listened. She needed to talk about her mother, and she didn't feel she could with you or Marge."

"She said that?"

"Yep."

"I didn't realize she felt that way."

"I think finding her mother's journal helped her let go of some of those emotions she's been holding inside."

"I know you and Ellie are coming out tomorrow for your riding lesson. Can you come a little later? I want to talk to Paige as soon as church is over." He backed out of the driveway and pointed his truck in the direction of Julia's apartment.

"I thought I would show you how to roast a hen as practice for that turkey on Thursday. Would three give you enough time?"

"Three sounds fine. You aren't going to come over and take pity on me and help with the Thanksgiving dinner?"

"Ah, now I realize why you asked me."

Her exaggerated exasperation made him laugh. "You found me out. I thought I was being real smooth."

"About as smooth as my first ride on your mare."

"That rough? I guess I'll have to work on my technique." He pulled up in front of her apartment building, not wanting the evening to end just yet. He angled toward her. "I hope you'll go to the movies with me another time."

"Are you asking me on a second date?"

"Yes." Although he couldn't see her face well because of the darkness, her teasing tone wiped any doubt he'd had that she wasn't interested.

He hadn't dated in a long time and was a bit rusty at it.

"When? I'll have to check my busy schedule."

"You pick."

"How about next Saturday night?"

"You've got yourself a date."

He clasped her shoulders and hauled her to him. His mouth claimed hers in a deep kiss. She felt so good in his arms.

"I'd better go now before…"

Determinedly, he set her away from him and wrenched open the door. After walking her to her apartment and giving her a chaste kiss on her cheek, he drove to his ranch.

He had some reading to do. After making a pot of strong coffee, he sat at the kitchen table and started at the beginning of Diane's diary. Two hours later he flipped the journal closed and stared at the wall across from him.

He hadn't realized how much his wife hated military life. Yes, they'd fought like all couples do, but it was usually over money or something to do with Paige, not his job. He'd known she hadn't been happy when his unit had been deployed to the Middle East, but most of the wives were upset their husbands would be gone for a year. Diane's feelings had been more than that.

The fact he'd been clueless unnerved him. What else had he missed? What was he missing now? He fingered the book, trying to decide how to present this to his daughter tomorrow. There were parts she was too young to understand, especially the section where his wife began taking drugs to numb herself.

He would focus on the pages about Paige and prayed that would satisfy his daughter.

Please, Father, help me get through this with Paige. My daughter is still trying to deal with her mother's death. She doesn't need to know all the ugly parts. Let her remember her mother in a good light. In Jesus Christ's name. Amen.

Paige settled next to Evan on the couch in the living room.

He opened the journal to the first page that mentioned his daughter and began reading.

"'My daughter walked for the first time today. I scooped her up and twirled her around. She loves that. Evan didn't get to see it, but I called him at the base and told him. When he came home later, he couldn't believe she could walk to him without holding on. Paige is only nine months! Before long she'll be running around here and I'll have to chase her. That'll be a great way to lose the last bit of pregnancy weight.'"

Evan started to turn to another section when Paige stopped him. "I walked at nine months?"

"Yep, and your mother was right. You started running around not long after that. You were active. You still are."

She released his arm. "Go on."

He read other passages and his daughter made a few comments, but as he came to the pages Diane wrote after she left Prairie Springs, Paige grew quiet.

"'I miss my daughter so much, but she's better off with her daddy. I wish I could hold her. She'll never know how much I really love her.'" Evan closed the diary.

His daughter's head hung down. When she peered up into his face, her eyes glistened with unshed tears. "If she loved me so much, then why did she leave me?"

The question he had been dreading to hear waited to be answered, and he wasn't sure what to say. He really didn't know the whole answer. He wasn't even sure Diane did. *So how do you tell your daughter that?*

"I'm not sure, princess."

His daughter stiffened, her hands balling in her lap.

"She didn't like her life here and decided she had to make a change."

Head still down, Paige murmured, "Why didn't she take me with her?"

"Because she knew how much I loved you, too. She thought you would be better off here."

"But she didn't come back to see me."

Because she got into drugs and lost control of her life. He couldn't tell Paige that—she needed to be older to hear that. He grappled with what to say.

Before he could come up with anything acceptable, Paige leaped to her feet. "She lied in that diary. She didn't really love me."

Evan reached for his daughter, but she eluded his grasp and raced out of the living room. He rose to go after her and somehow make her understand. The back door slammed shut.

By the time he left his house, Julia had pulled up in back and Ellie and Paige were running toward the barn.

Julia's forehead creased with concern as she came up to him. "Paige was crying. Ellie went to see what's wrong."

"I read parts of Diane's diary to her, but only

the sections about her and in those her mother kept talking about how much she loved her daughter. Paige couldn't understand why she left then."

"Why did she?"

He recited all the reasons he'd gleaned from the journal in a monotone voice. "She hated the life she was living. She wanted nothing to do with being a military wife. She'd even forgotten why we married in the first place. By the time she left, the only good thing that came out of our marriage was Paige."

Julia covered his hands. "I'm sorry this is being dragged up again. It can't be easy."

"Diane is behind me. What upsets me now is what this is doing to my daughter."

Julia studied his face, his jaw set in a hard line. Was he really over his wife? His anger vibrated off him. "Let Paige calm down and then talk to her again. Give her time—and yourself, too."

He stared down at his fists. "I guess you're right." Sitting on the back step where he could see the entrance into the barn, he scooted over to give her room to ease down next to him. "I'll give Paige and Ellie fifteen minutes, then we're going to find them."

* * *

"Paige, what's wrong?" Ellie plopped down on the pile of hay in one of the empty stalls.

"My mommy—didn't love me. She—" Paige hiccuped "—left me."

Ellie put her arm around her friend. "I never knew my daddy, but Mommy said he loved me." She remembered her mother adding, "How could he not love such an adorable little girl."

Swiping her cheeks, Paige glanced at Ellie. "Then why did he leave?"

"He didn't love my mommy enough to stay. But Mommy said that had nothing to do with me." Ellie grinned. "Mommy loves me enough for both of them. She told me that and she does."

Sniffing, Paige cocked her head to the side. "Yeah, Daddy loves me bunches. But I want a mommy."

"I know." Ellie rested her chin in her palm. "I want a daddy. Do you think my mommy and your daddy will marry?"

"I hope so. Then we could be sisters." Paige scrunched her face into a thoughtful look. "But we may have to help them."

"How?"

"I don't know. We'll think of something."

"Paige. Ellie. Where are you?" Evan shouted.

Ellie and Paige jumped to their feet and peeked over the half door toward the entrance into the barn.

"We're here." Ellie waved, then whispered to Paige. "Wouldn't it be nice if we were a family by Christmas?"

"That would be the best present ever." Paige snatched a piece of straw from Ellie's hair.

When Julia arrived at the stall, the girls emerged. "Are you two ready to go riding?"

Evan knelt in front of his daughter. "Are you all right, princess?"

Paige threw her arms around his neck and kissed him on the cheek. "I love ya."

Scooping his daughter up into his embrace, Evan rose. "I love you. I don't want you to be unhappy."

"I know, Daddy. You have enough love for Mommy and you." Paige laid her head on his shoulder. "Ellie explained everything."

He smiled at her. "Well then, Ellie, you get to ride extra long today."

Jumping up and down, she clapped. "That's the second best present you could give me."

"What's the first?" her mother asked, taking her hand and strolling toward Bessie's stall.

"It's a secret."

* * *

"Not bad, Daddy." Paige carried her plate over to the sink.

Evan caught Julia's gaze. "I wish I could take credit for the roasted hen, but mostly I watched Julia. I did make the green beans and rice, though." Which entailed following the simple directions—that even he could understand—on the rice box.

"Can we watch TV?" His daughter pushed in her chair.

"That's fine. I'll clean up tonight."

Ellie grabbed her dishes and put them on the counter, then hurried toward the hallway.

"After I help Evan clean up, we'll need to go home, Ellie," Julia said right before her daughter disappeared from the kitchen.

"It's only seven o'clock."

"Tomorrow is a school day, and I have to go to work early. It's a short week with Thanksgiving." Julia gathered up what was left on the table and brought it to the sink.

When she turned back toward Evan, he was right behind her and trapped her against the counter, his arms caging her. "This will be the first Thanksgiving I'm actually looking forward to in several years."

"Because you're gonna fix the meal?" Her eyes danced with mischief.

He tweaked her nose, then followed it with a quick kiss. "I don't think so."

"Because your daughter is happy?"

"I'm happy she is happy, but that's not it, either."

Julia peered over Evan's shoulder, then whispered, "Because you're going to have the dinner here, not at Marge's?"

He chuckled. "My mother-in-law and I are coming to an understanding finally." Slipping his arms around her, he nestled closer. "So guess again."

"I give up."

"You. I've come to appreciate Thanksgiving again. I'm looking forward to sharing it with you and Ellie. Our girls get along so well and we do, too." With tiny kisses he teased the corners of her mouth. "And the fact that I'm sure you'll help me with dinner, since you'll have to eat it."

Julia exaggerated a pout. "I knew it! That's the real reason I was invited."

"If you really think that, I'll just have to convince you otherwise." His lips hovered above hers.

The ringing of the home phone startled Evan. He jumped back and swung around toward it. As he snatched it up, he sent Julia a smile and mouthed the words, "Don't go anywhere."

"Paterson here."

"Evan, this is Mike Montgomery."

Evan tensed, the smile on his lips dying. "Have they found Whitney?" Dr. Mike Montgomery was one of the people keeping him informed about the search for his sister. He didn't want a car to pull up at his ranch with unfamiliar army personnel in it to deliver bad news.

"They've found a mass grave. It's where they thought she might be."

Chapter Ten

Stunned, Evan barely made it to the desk chair and collapsed into it. His hands trembled, and all color drained from his face.

"Please let me know as soon as you hear. I appreciate the heads-up." After replacing the phone in its cradle, he stared down at it, unmoving as though paralyzed.

Julia ached for him and wished she could take some of his pain away. Julia laid a comforting hand on his shoulder. "Did they find Whitney?"

He didn't say anything for a long moment. She wasn't even sure he heard her. Then he swept around, pain etched into his ashen features.

"They found her dog tags in a mass grave of charred bodies. There's one that fits her build. They are running tests to see if it's her."

"It might not be."

"A soldier doesn't part with their dog tags willingly." He plowed his hands through his hair. "What am I going to do? What am I going to say to Paige?"

"Pray, and say nothing until they confirm it is Whitney."

"I've been praying for my sister's safe return for months. I guess God's answer is no. Why? She was a good Christian. She was a much better person than I am and I'm still alive." He thumped his chest as though to emphasize that fact.

"I don't have an easy answer. I know that God sometimes tells us no to our requests, and we often never know why. We're His children and like any child we don't always understand the reason behind a parent's denial." Julia clasped his upper arms. "Remember He told Jesus no at Gethsemane. Christ said, 'My Father, if it is not possible for this cup to be taken away unless I drink it, may Your will be done.'"

He wrenched away. "I don't want to deal with any more death."

There was anguish in his voice. She searched for a way to help him but could think of nothing beyond what she had already said. He wasn't hearing her words right now. He'd buried himself in his past.

"Do you want me to see if Paige will go home with us and spend the night with Ellie?"

"No! I need my daughter close."

She wanted to ask him, "Do you think that's wise?" when he said, "It's getting late. I'll clean up later."

"I'll get Ellie and we'll go, but Evan, remember I'm only a phone call away. If you need to talk, call me no matter what time it is."

A slight nod was the only acknowledgement that he had heard her. She called to Ellie to get her things, that they were leaving. Both girls came running into the kitchen, disappointment on their faces.

"Why so early?" Ellie asked in a whining voice.

"Because there's a lot to be done this week. Remember the big Thanksgiving feast your class is participating in on Wednesday? You two will be busy tomorrow and the next day at school." Julia gathered up her purse, aware that Evan's expression held no hint of what had transpired a few minutes before in the kitchen. He hid his pain well.

"You're comin' to the feast, aren't ya?" Paige peered at Julia then Evan.

"Yes," Julia said while Evan nodded.

"Wait till you see the place mats we made for the parents."

Paige waved Ellie quiet. "That's supposed to be a surprise."

"Oh, I forgot." Her daughter's face colored a cherry red.

"Thanks for the riding lesson and dinner," Julia said as she crossed the room.

Outside on the stoop she heard Paige say, "Why are the dishes still dirty, Daddy?"

Closing the back door, she missed Evan's reply. She so badly wanted to linger, to be there for him, but he had made it very clear he didn't want her around. He was shutting her out, retreating within himself. Her own pain mingled with his as she slowly descended the steps.

"Mommy, what's wrong?"

She stopped under the glow of the security light and faced her daughter. "Nothing a hug from you won't make better."

Ellie flung her arms around Julia's waist and embraced her so tightly that it affected her breathing. She eased back and bent to kiss her daughter on the top of her head.

"Let's go home." Julia offered Ellie her hand, and they strolled to the car.

As Julia put the car into Drive, she glanced at the house and saw Evan silhouetted in the kitchen window. His head dropped forward while he leaned into the table as though it was the only thing that held him upright.

He stared down into the dark hole. Glimpses of his sister zoomed in and out of focus. Kneeling, he reached into the blackness. He grasped a rope and tugged on it. Whitney loomed before him. He pulled faster.

The hole shrank until there was nothing before him but solid ground. He pounded his fists into the earth.

"Whitney! Come back."

Body shaking, Evan bolted up in bed, his heart pounding. He swiped his arm across his wet forehead and sank back against the headboard. The rasp of his breathing echoed in the quiet of the house.

The darkness surrounding him, like the hole in his dream, taunted him. Who was he kidding? Missing for months. He had to prepare himself for the worst.

Finally, his heartbeat slowed its quick pace, but there would be no sleep for him the rest of the night. Kicking the sheet off him, Evan sat on the edge of the mattress, his phone sitting on the table nearby. Julia was only a call away. She said she would listen to him talk day or night. All he had to do was pick up the receiver and open himself up to her. His fingertips traced the plastic length. He even lifted the phone from its base.

Open himself up to her. Like a wound. Bleeding all over her. She didn't deserve all his baggage. He slammed the handset back into the base and padded into the hallway.

As he passed Paige's room, he paused and pushed open her door. Her curtains revealed a sliver of moonlight that cast its light across her still form, nestled under her covers.

He moved toward her. How was he going to tell his daughter yet another loved one in her life had died? When she had heard about Ali's grandfather, she had retreated into silence for hours and wouldn't tell him what was bothering her.

Why, Lord? Just tell me why. Make me understand Your plan.

"Thanks, Sarah, for dragging Ellie and me here tonight. I needed this." Julia sat on the bench next to her friend, who was also Ellie's teacher.

"When I saw you this morning dropping your daughter off, I knew something was wrong."

"I looked that bad?" After running her fingers through her hair, Julia tucked a lock of it behind her ears.

"I can tell when something is wrong and you need someone to talk to. Must be the teacher in me."

"I'm so glad you're Ellie's." Julia gestured toward her daughter and Ali playing the games for the children at the pizza parlor. "And Ali will be blessed to have you as a mother."

Sarah's blue eyes glinted. Her mouth tightened into a frown. "He's been through so much. But look, your daughter makes him laugh."

Ali tried to roll a ball into a hole, but it bounced out. Ellie retrieved it and gave it to him to do again.

"But we didn't come here for me or Ali, Julia. What's wrong?"

"What you saw this morning was someone who hadn't gotten more than an hour or two of sleep last night."

Ellie ran up to her. "Mommy, I need more tickets. Me and Ali are gonna be over there." Her daughter pointed toward a huge ride with different kinds of cars that went around in a circle.

"This is it. So use them wisely." Julia dug

into her purse and retrieved the last ones she had purchased.

"Here's Ali's." Sarah gave Ellie the boy's tickets.

"It doesn't take them long to go through five dollars' worth."

Her daughter hurried back to Ali and took his hand to guide him to the ride. She remembered when he had first seen the large play area at the back of the family restaurant. Now that he was feeling better, he was experiencing and enjoying a lot more. But as with Evan, she still saw in his eyes the loss he had gone through.

Julia was falling in love—again—with a man who was relationship shy. Evan had been clear from the beginning that he didn't want to get married again. With Clayton she had found out after she had discovered she was pregnant. She should be thankful for Evan's honesty, but it didn't take away the hurt.

Julia confided in Sarah. "Evan found out that his sister might be one of the bodies the army found in a mass grave. Mike Montgomery called him last night to let him know what happened."

"Mike?" Sarah whispered, then straightening as though pulling herself together, she continued, "You said might. Is there any doubt?"

"The bodies were charred, but her dog tags were there. The army is running tests to determine if it's Whitney."

"Poor Evan. This must be awful for him. These past few months have been such a trial."

"Mike told him he would call back as soon as he found out anything. But that could be a while." A shutter fell over Sarah's features, and Julia couldn't ignore the reaction any longer. "I'm sorry about you and Mike."

"That was a long time ago, and I've moved on. I have Ali to think about now."

Sarah sounded like her. When Ellie was born, she had told herself all she needed was her daughter. Getting involved with a man wouldn't complete her life, that she was better off without Clayton. She now believed that yes she was better off without her college boyfriend, but she also realized her life wasn't complete. There was something missing, and she was afraid it was Evan. A man she couldn't have.

Sarah unclasped her hands and flexed her fingers. "You are good. I see you're avoiding why we are here. I asked you to dinner tonight to help you, and we're talking about me. A dull subject, if you ask me." Her laughter vied with the clangs and whistles of the various games. "Were you able to help Evan any?"

"No. He practically threw me out after he got the call." He had listened to her when she had talked about Clayton but hadn't let her help him when he needed someone. The thought sank the hurt deeper into her heart.

"Some men have trouble expressing their emotions."

Was Sarah talking about Evan or Mike? Probably both, Julia decided. And even if Evan loved her, she couldn't be in a relationship with him if he couldn't share himself totally with her. When she thought back to hers with Clayton, that had been the problem. She'd shared her life with him but not the other way around.

Ellie and Ali climbed out of their cars and headed toward them. Julia stood, gathering up her purse. "When I marry, it will be with a man who loves me enough to include me in the bad as well as the good parts of his life. I want to be his best friend and lover."

Julia stepped into the elementary school cafeteria and searched for her daughter. Parents stood or sat with their children at the tables that filled the large room.

"You're here finally!" Ellie rushed toward her. "I didn't think you were coming. Everyone else is here already."

"I'm sorry, honey. I got caught up at the office."

Her daughter tugged on her hand, dragging her across the cafeteria. "I've got our place over here next to Paige and her dad."

Spying the pair already at the table, she nearly pulled her hand free from Ellie's. She wasn't sure she could handle seeing Evan when he hadn't phoned, not that he owed her a call. But each hour she hadn't heard from him reconfirmed in her mind that he wanted to remain alone. After Clayton, she knew she needed to cut her losses now before she couldn't mend her heart.

"Mommy?"

Julia stared into her daughter's worried face, then she noticed that she had slowed so much she had come to a stop. To avoid an explanation, she decided to make a production out of viewing the decorations the children had made for the Thanksgiving feast. She said, "You all have been working so hard."

"C'mon. I'll show you what our class made." Again Ellie pulled her through the milling parents with their children until she arrived at the table where Evan and Paige sat. "Me and Paige made the centerpiece and the place mats there." She pointed toward a large turkey made out of various vegetables and fruits.

"And we also helped—" Paige hopped to her feet and patted the wall nearby with a large mural of the first Thanksgiving hanging on it "—with coloring the sky and I even got to color the dress on that pilgrim."

"Paige colors better than me, but I'm the best cutter in the class." Ellie thrust out her chest. "See my feathers on the turkey?"

Julia avoided Evan's gaze and eased onto the undersized chair, grateful she wore pants since her knees were practically in her chest. "I love this turkey place mat. Will we get to take them home and use them tomorrow?"

Ellie nodded and settled into the chair next to Julia. "Because we are the youngest, we get to go first." Her daughter leaned toward her and whispered in a voice loud enough they could hear at the next table, "The big kids have to wait to last to go through the line."

"Well, munchkin, you'll be a big kid one day and have to wait."

Ellie grinned. "But not this year and I'm starved."

"So am I."

Julia glanced toward Paige, who had spoken, and in the process caught Evan's gaze on her. Her breath caught in her throat. Although there were so many people around them, for a moment she and Evan were the only ones in the room. He averted his attention to the principal standing at the front of the room.

Julia's gaze lingered on Evan, his vulnerability holding her captive. She had to reach him somehow. Finally, she turned back to the woman in front who was asking the crowd for a moment of silence.

Julia bowed her head and whispered so only those closest to her would hear, "Father, bless this food we are about to partake. Show us Your will and guide us in Your way. In Jesus Christ's name. Amen."

Quickly the children and parents at the kindergarten table filed through the serving line and returned with turkey, dressing, green-bean casserole and pumpkin pie.

Sarah sat at the head of table with Ali next to her. After she got everyone's attention, she said, "I would like y'all to say one thing you're thankful for this Thanksgiving. I will start. I am thankful for Ali's presence in my life."

"I'm thankful for my friends and learning to ride a horse," Ellie said when it was her turn.

All eyes turned to Julia next. "That's easy. I'm thankful for my daughter."

Ellie gave Julia a hug as the person beside her spoke. "Mommy, I'm always thankful for you," Ellie whispered into Julia's ear.

"I know, honey."

When it reached Paige, the little girl's eyes danced with mischief. "I'm thankful that my daddy is friends with Julia."

Evan coughed, his face red. He murmured something to Paige.

She grinned. "But I am, Daddy."

Everyone stared at Evan, whose embarrassment grew. He opened his mouth to say something, decided not to and waved his hand toward the person next to him. Julia dropped her gaze to her plate, feeling the weight of a few people's eyes on her. She was thankful when it was time to eat. She dug into her food as though she had been fasting for forty days, afraid to glance across the table at Evan.

"Daddy, can I spend the night at Ellie's tonight?"

"Tonight?"

"You said anytime I was ready to sleep over at a friend's you would let me."

"I did?"

Julia heard the doubt in his voice and looked up. "Maybe some other—"

"Mommy, we won't be a problem at all tonight. We've got plans. Please." Ellie's gaze shifted from Julia to Evan. "Please."

Julia finally peered at Evan. "It's all right with me. We can come over early tomorrow, and I'll help you with making the dinner."

"Fine then."

His stiff tone told her that it really wasn't. "Are you sure?"

He nodded once.

The tension emanating from Evan made it hard for Julia to finish her meal. Maybe it would be better if she and Ellie had Thanksgiving by themselves. But beneath his facade she saw he was hurting. She wanted to help, even if he didn't want her to. She needed to talk to him.

Thirty minutes later as the parents were leaving, Julia hurried to catch up with Evan, whose long-legged pace was quickly chewing up the distance between the school and his truck.

"Evan."

He turned toward her, that bland look on his face.

"Why don't you let me take care of Thanksgiving dinner? We can have it at my place." Her breath came out in pants.

"No, I've already bought everything. The turkey is in my refrigerator thawing right now. Paige is looking forward to it."

"But not you."

In frustration he kneaded his nape. "I'll put on a good show for my daughter. I don't want her to hear anything about Whitney until I know for sure."

"So nothing yet?"

"Mike said it would take some time, but he would push to get it done as quickly as possible."

"What time would you like us to show up tomorrow?"

"Eight or nine. I should be able to get the turkey in without any problem, but beyond that I don't know." One corner of his mouth lifted.

"Then we'll be there bright and early and ready to work." She moved closer to him, aware the parking lot was emptying of parents who had taken their lunch break to eat with their child. "What about Paige's pajamas, a change of clothing?"

"I'll bring them by later this afternoon. When will you be home?"

"I'm going to my apartment right now. I have the rest of the day off. I told Ellie I would pick her and Paige up after school, otherwise I'll be there."

"Then I'll see you later." He climbed into his truck without another word.

Julia crossed the parking lot to her car. As she left, she noticed that Evan was still sitting in his truck, his head resting on the steering wheel. She almost turned around, then remembered the closed look he gave her as he got into his pickup. She needed to talk to someone. She didn't know what to do.

"I'm sorry that the reverend is not here, Julia. He should be back later this afternoon." Olga closed the door to the grief center at the church. "Can I be of any help?" she asked as she started walking down the hallway.

Julia hesitated, causing the older woman to turn toward her. "I…" Knowing how Olga loved to play matchmaker, she didn't think she should say anything to her.

"This is about Evan?"

Olga's assessing gaze pinned Julia down.

Cornered and not sure what to tell her, she nodded, her throat closed.

"Evan reminds me of the reverend."

"He does?"

"Neither one knows a good thing when he sees it—or rather a good woman. Don't give up on him, Julia. He needs you even if he doesn't see that right now." Olga lifted her arms up in an exaggerated shrug. "Now if only I can take my own advice."

"About Reverend Fields?"

The older woman laughed. "Lately everything seems to be about that man." She began heading toward the side door again. "Come back later this afternoon after three. Hopefully he will be back by then."

Julia started to follow the woman out of the building, stopped halfway to the door and changed direction. She made her way toward the sanctuary. Sitting in the front pew, she bowed her head and prayed to the Lord.

Father, what do I do about Evan?

She opened her heart for an answer but none came. Minutes ticked into half an hour, and still there was no solution. Although she loved Evan, praying hadn't made anything clearer—in fact, she was even more confused than before.

Finally, because she had told Evan she would be at her apartment so he could drop off Paige's clothes, she rose and strode toward the door in back that led to the foyer. Something drew her attention toward one of the hallways off the main entrance. Olga had created a Wall of Hope with letters and pictures from children to military personnel stationed in the Middle East and from the soldiers to the kids.

Through the slightly open door she spied Evan reading the copies of letters taped to the wall up and down the hall. At first she thought about leaving, then she saw him wipe his eyes, and she couldn't. He sank down on the bench across from the section of the wall devoted to his sister and her husband and buried his face in his hands.

His pain reached out and beckoned her.

"Evan," she whispered in the quiet, her voice raspy with her own emotions.

He stiffened, then lifted his gaze to hers. "Have you ever read these?" He gestured toward the letters.

Shaking her head, she stepped closer.

"They are writing about Whitney and John and about how they hope they are found soon.

Thankfully, John has been, but…" His voice faded into the silence, his face averted.

"He still hasn't remembered anything?"

"No, not much. I talked to him last night. Mike had also called him in Germany about the body. He was…" Sadness roughened his tone, his eyes glistening. He cleared his throat and continued. "These children have been praying to God for my sister to come home. Letter after letter. Their prayers are in vain."

"Are they? You don't know that."

"No, but…" He swallowed hard.

"If it hasn't been confirmed it was Whitney, then there is hope. That's what these children are writing about. And if the Lord has decided to bring your sister home to Him, then we have to trust in His reason."

"So until I hear otherwise, I should think my sister is alive?"

"Why not?"

He turned away. "I wish it was that simple."

She came to him and touched his arm. "It is that simple. You shouldn't grieve before you know for sure. That's a wasted emotion."

"You obviously see a glass half-full, not half-empty."

Smiling, she sat next to him on the bench. "I

try. I don't always succeed. Besides, Paige will sense something is wrong. She's a very smart little girl."

"That's why I agreed to having her spend the night with Ellie. I didn't think I could keep up my front much longer."

"Then how are you going to make it through Thanksgiving dinner?"

He shrugged. "I hadn't thought that far in advance. Maybe Mike will call me before then." He fingered a piece of paper near him. "There are a lot of people who care about what happens to my sister and her husband."

"Yes, you aren't alone in this, and if you find out that it is Whitney, you need to remember that. I am here for you. The Lord is here for you." Julia took his hand, hoping to convey some of her support through her touch.

"I'm trying. It's just not been easy. I've held dying men, people who fought beside me and were taken while I lived. I was there when they took their last breath. I started asking the question—why did they die and why did I live? I don't have an answer to that." His fingers about hers tightened. "Why Whitney and not me?"

"Only God can answer that. We just have to

trust and put our will into His hands. He sees the bigger picture. We don't."

"Blind faith?"

"Faith is believing in something we can't see. We just know in our mind and heart it is real."

"I don't know if I have it in me anymore." Resting his elbows on his thighs, he hunched his shoulders in defeat. "I shouldn't be here."

Julia strained to hear his faint words. "Of course you should. This is about your sister." She waved her hand toward the area of the wall concerning Whitney.

"No, I mean I should…" He closed his eyes. "Right before I was to come home, we went on patrol. I should have gone into the building first, but instead one of my men did. He tripped a bomb and was killed instantly. That was supposed to be me, but I had stopped to radio our position back to the base camp. Something didn't feel right." Evan scrubbed his hands down his face. "Before I had a chance to tell Mac to wait, he entered the building. He had a wife and kid back home. I…"

The heartache in his voice knifed through her. She stroked his arm. "I'm so sorry, Evan. But you weren't at fault—"

He rounded on her. "Not my fault? If I had

said something about my gut feeling before radioing our location, Mac would still be alive today. I have to live with the guilt. Coming here was a mistake." He bolted to his feet, a trapped look appearing in his eyes, as if the deluge of memories was overpowering.

Julia slowly rose. "You didn't kill Mac. It wasn't your time."

Evan scanned the length of both walls, filled with letters and photos. "Let's go. I need to get Paige's clothes, and the girls will need to be picked up soon."

Before she had a chance to say anything else about the guilt he was experiencing, Evan had left the hallway. She hurried to catch up with him. But his stony expression forbade any further discussion.

Evan stopped at his truck and opened his door.

Julia couldn't leave him that way. Torment shadowed his eyes. "Feeling guilty won't bring Mac back. You're alive because the Lord wants you alive. Ask yourself why He does. What are you supposed to do with your life?"

In silence he climbed into his pickup, started his engine and left the parking lot.

He was hurt, and she didn't know if she would be able to help him.

Chapter Eleven

"This is a surprise. What brings you by this afternoon?" Julia swung the door wide open for Sarah and Ali to come into her apartment.

"This." Sarah held up one of Ellie's place mats. "She left it at school, and I wanted her to have both of them for tomorrow's Thanksgiving meal."

Julia took it. "I really appreciate this. I hope you two will stay for a while."

"You haven't started cooking for Thanksgiving?"

"I'm not cooking this year. Well, I am baking a couple of pies, but that's all." Julia turned to Ali. "Why don't you go find Ellie and Paige? They're in Ellie's bedroom playing." She crossed the living room with the little boy to show him where to go.

The girls' squeals proceeded Ellie proclaiming in a loud voice, "Oh, good, now we have someone to be the daddy."

Julia chuckled. "Poor Ali. He may never be the same. Let's go into the kitchen. I've got some water on the stove. Would you like a cup of tea or something else to drink?"

"Tea sounds fine." Sarah glanced toward the hallway when sounds of giggles drifted from Ellie's bedroom. "I imagine Ali's had a lot of firsts since coming to America."

"I'm so glad to see he's getting stronger."

"With each day he has more energy." Sarah sat at the table. "Mmm. You must be baking a pumpkin pie."

"Of course. It's a must for Thanksgiving, but I also have a chocolate one, since Evan loves it."

"You're having dinner with him tomorrow?"

"Yes, Ellie and I are." Julia retrieved two cups from the cabinet and poured hot water into each one.

"He's cooking? I thought his mother-in-law made most of his meals?"

The incredulous tone in Sarah's voice made Julia laugh. "I told him I would come early and help, but he's going to do a lot of the work. I've been teaching him how to cook."

"You have! My, you two have been getting close."

"And he's been teaching Ellie how to ride. She loves horses."

"What little girl doesn't?"

Julia set a cup before Sarah. "This one. Pets and animals were never big at my house when I was growing up so I never thought of having a horse. But Evan is teaching me to ride, too." She settled in a chair across from her friend.

"Interesting. Do you realize every other word from you is about Evan?"

Although steam wafted from her cup, the heat that flooded Julia's face was from something else. "We have been seeing a lot of each other but…" She grappled with what to say next. She loved Evan, but after today at the Wall of Hope, she didn't have much hope that he would ever really let her into his life.

"But what?" Sarah sipped her tea.

"I really l-like him, but I don't think there's a future for us." There, she had said it out loud.

"Do you think he's still mourning his deceased wife?"

"I don't know. He's wrestling with a lot right now." Julia cradled the hot cup between her palms. "I don't want to be hurt again, and I certainly don't want my daughter to be, either."

Sarah's eyes narrowed. "Do you love Evan?"

"You really cut right to the chase, don't you?" Julia blew a breath out between pursed lips. "It doesn't make any difference how I feel."

"Yes, it does." Sarah leaned forward. "You need to fight for the relationship if you love him."

"I have more than myself to consider. Ellie already looks forward to seeing Evan. I don't want her to start dreaming of having a family then have it all blow up in her face. She's been through enough with my parents and Clayton."

"I thought your mom's visit went well."

"She calls and spends a lot of time talking to Ellie, but my father still hasn't spoken one word to me or Ellie. As stubborn as he is, I doubt that's going to change."

"What does Ellie say?"

"Not much now. But there were times in Chicago when I found her crying. She wanted to know about her daddy. I told her the truth. I don't know where he is, that he left me, not her." Julia took a drink of her tea. "But she's always wanted a daddy. I've tried to be both a mother and father to Ellie. But it's not the same thing."

Sarah sighed. "I guess I'll be facing that

problem with Ali. Although our circumstances are different, I'll be raising him as a single mom, like you and Ellie."

"I thought that Evan and I could be friends, but I can't do it anymore." Not seeing him would hurt, but for her daughter's happiness she had to steel herself against the pain and move on. "I want more than friendship, and he isn't capable of giving more. After tomorrow I'll be seeing a lot less of him. I've got to protect my heart and Ellie's."

"I know all about protecting the heart, so I guess I can't say too much to you."

"A mother has to do what's best for the family." But as Julia said the words, her heart cracked at the thought of not seeing Evan. The past month had given her a taste of what a whole family could be like.

Evan took the twenty-pound turkey out of the refrigerator and stared at it. What in the world was he supposed to do with it? Read the directions. That was the first thing Julia had taught him. Then take it one step at a time. Okay, he could do this.

He set the turkey on the counter next to the sink and pushed into it to see if it was still frozen. His thumb met resistance. Frozen solid. Great, so now what was he supposed to do? It needed to be in the oven in less than twelve hours. At the rate the meat was thawing, he could start cooking Friday at seven, not Thursday. He shouldn't have gotten such a large bird, but he loved leftovers.

Think! How can I get twenty pounds of meat thawed fast? Microwave? No, it's too big. Won't fit. Hair dryer? No. Hot water? That's it!

He'd set it in hot water in the sink. As he ran the tap, he thought back to the afternoon with Julia. He couldn't give her what she wanted. Guilt riddled him, and he didn't know how to let it go.

For the past few years he had tried to forget. He'd seen so many soldiers die, some friends, and yet he had walked away unscathed. And now his sister was a victim.

But it wasn't just survivor's guilt. He had let Diane down, too. Would she be alive today if he had not been in the military and shipped overseas?

The blare of the phone cut into his thoughts. He quickly turned off the hot water and hurried to answer. "Hello."

"Evan—the girls are gone."

There was panic in Julia's voice. "Gone? What do you mean?"

"After Sarah and Ali left a little while ago, they went back in Ellie's room to watch a movie. When I called them to dinner, they didn't come. I—"

"Didn't come?"

"I've checked the whole apartment. They aren't here and—"

"Are you sure they aren't hiding somewhere in the—"

"No, they aren't, and they aren't in the hallway or next door with Ellie's babysitter."

"What about outside?" His tight grip on the receiver sent pain shooting up his arm.

"It's dark. Ellie knows she can't go…" A long pause and a deep breath accompanied the silence. "I'll go check and call you back."

"I'm coming over."

"But they may—"

"I'm coming over. Call me on my cell." He slammed down the phone, snatched up the keys and raced for his truck.

He flew down the dirt road to the highway, the jarring of the truck chattering his teeth. Heading into town, he pushed the speedometer above the lawful limit.

When his cell phone rang, he flipped it open. "Were they there?"

"No, not a sign of them."

"I'll be there in ten minutes. Check with all your neighbors." He clicked off and concentrated on the road, accelerating even more.

He couldn't lose his daughter. He had so little to hold on to right now.

"Look, all the lights are on." Poking her arm out of the large hedge they hid in, Paige pointed toward the very large Victorian house where Ellie's apartment was.

"When do you think your dad will be here?" Ellie hugged the blanket closer around her jacket to keep the cold night air out.

"Soon. I hope this works like in *The Parent Trap*."

"Me, too. They just need to be together more, then they will love each other."

Paige snuggled under the blanket against Ellie. "I don't understand why they are mad at each other."

"Mommy said she wasn't gonna see your daddy after tomorrow. I want a daddy."

"Yeah. Your mommy is so nice. They'll see we belong together. You just wait and see."

"I hope it's soon. It's cold." Ellie's teeth chattered, and she burrowed even closer to her friend. "When will we know it's time to go home?"

"We'll know."

Although Paige sounded sure, her voice wavered. Ellie wasn't so positive everything would turn out as in the movie.

Julia paced the porch, biting her nails, something she hadn't done in a long time. The screech of tires drew her attention to the street. Evan slammed to a stop in front and leaped from his truck. As he marched toward her, his determined expression froze her.

"Have you checked everywhere around here?" he asked before she could say anything.

"Yes. No one has seen the girls. Should we call the police?" Images of Paige and Ellie, small and vulnerable, paraded across her mind.

"Maybe. Where were they last?"

"In Ellie's room watching a movie."

"Show me."

His clipped tone rivaled the cold weather. She hurried into the house and mounted the stairs to the second floor. The hairs on her nape stood up. He acted as though she had purposely lost their daughters. Tears swelled into her eyes.

He searched Ellie's bedroom, picking up the DVD of the movie the children were watching. The censure of his gaze sliced to her.

"Where were you?"

The sting of the question bit into her. "I was here." Her voice rose as she indicated in the apartment. "Do you think I left them alone?"

For a few seconds the hardness in his eyes continued to intimidate her, then something deflated in him. He dropped onto Ellie's bed, shaking his head. "I know you didn't." His shoulders slumped as he clutched his hands. "It doesn't look like anyone came in here and took them, which probably means they snuck off somewhere."

"Where? They knew I was fixing dinner." Her legs could no longer hold her up. She sat, too, as far away from him as she possibly could on a twin bed.

"I don't know. A friend's. You said something about Sarah and Ali stopping by. Do you think they went over there?"

"Sarah would call me if they had, but I'll check with her anyway."

"I'll make a few calls, too, then we'll call the police."

She sucked in a deep breath.

"Just to be on the safe side. Even if they went off on their own, they could get into trouble."

Julia went into the living room and dialed Sarah's number. After discovering the girls weren't there, she phoned a couple of more people to see if they had seen Ellie and Paige, but no one had. She walked back into Ellie's bedroom as Evan snapped his cell phone closed.

The bleak look on his face told her all she needed to know. He hadn't done any better than she had.

"I'll inform the police." Evan flipped open his cell again. "Like I said, no telling what could happen to two little girls out by themselves at night."

Different scenarios flashed through Julia's mind as Evan talked with the police. What if they fell and hurt themselves? What if the wrong person found them or offered them a ride? She shuddered. Crossing her arms, she hugged herself, but the cold drove straight into her heart.

"They'll be here shortly."

She saw Evan through a blur of tears. She couldn't shake the terrible images from her mind. They clung to her like glue.

In two strides he stood in front of her, gripping her arms. "Julia, we should wait downstairs for them." When she didn't reply, he tilted her face up toward his. "We'll find them."

His blurry image shimmered. "I'm sorry. I'm sorry. I should have watched them better."

"No, they should have stayed where they were supposed to. I don't know what they were thinking."

A tear leaked out and ran down her cheek. "They weren't. This isn't like Ellie."

"Paige, either." He brushed the pad of his thumb across her face. "We'll find them."

"I think I know why they snuck out." She gestured toward the DVD of *The Parent Trap* lying on the bed. "I believe they're trying to bring us together, like in the movie."

Pulling back, but still holding her loosely, he said, "I don't understand."

The ringing of the chimes jolted Julia. She wrenched free and hurried into the living room. When she opened the door, she started to say Ellie's name, but it instantly died on her lips as she faced her neighbor, Ruth.

"Did you find Ellie and Paige?" her daughter's babysitter asked.

"No. We called the police."

"Oh, dear. I'm here to help you look for them."

Another tenant in the apartment house came down the hall. "I'm here to help, too." The elderly man who lived downstairs buttoned his heavy coat.

Julia glanced back at Evan. "We're going

outside to look some more and wait for the police."

The young woman who lived on the other side of Julia joined the small group gathering. "Then we'll search, too."

When Julia emerged from the house, Sarah, Anna and David approached the house. Another car pulled up to the curb.

"Mom would have been here, but she volunteered to watch Ali so Sarah could help look for the girls." Anna paused at the bottom of the steps.

Evan stood next to Julia, clasping her hand. She would draw comfort from his presence for the time being, but once the girls were found, safe and sound, she would put an end to their relationship. She couldn't do it anymore. Not when her daughter was going to such extremes to bring her and Evan together. It would be better if Ellie was disappointed now rather than when she would have more hope vested in the relationship later.

Behind the small crowd forming in the yard, a police car parked at the end of the driveway, and two officers climbed from it. When she saw them striding up the walk, Julia tightened her grip on Evan's hand. For a moment the appearance of the police underscored all the things that could happen to the children.

Father, please bring the girls home safely. Let me be right and the only reason they ran away was to bring Evan and me together.

Ellie yanked on Paige's shirt. "Look! The police!"

"Shh. Let me think," Paige whispered into Ellie's ear. "We can't let them find us hiding here."

"Why not?"

"Then Daddy and your mommy will figure out what we're doing."

Ellie stared at the scene across the street. The officers mounted the steps and began talking to Julia. She shook her head, then looked at Evan. Paige's daddy waved behind him toward the house. Then all four of them went inside while everyone else stayed outside.

"Let's go." Paige shrugged out of the blanket.

"Where?"

"To the park at the town green."

"Why?" Ellie glanced back at her home.

"They'll find us at the park playing. They'll think we wanted to go and play at the park, not get them together. We've got to go now before they come back outside."

"I don't know. The police! We're gonna be in big trouble."

"We're already in big trouble. We don't wanna make it worse. My daddy never likes to be forced into anything."

"My mommy doesn't, either."

"See, so we've got to go to the park. It's only a couple of blocks from here."

"But it's dark."

Paige crawled out from their hiding place and stood behind the hedge so no one could see her. She held her hand out for Ellie. "We'll be okay if we stick together."

She scooted out, leaving the blanket. Beneath her friend's brave words, doubt rang. *Maybe Paige is right.* Through an opening in the hedge, Ellie looked across the street. *I hope she is. If this works, I'll finally have a daddy.*

Julia swept her arm across her body to indicate Ellie's room. "This was where they were, officer. I was in the kitchen the whole time. I didn't hear anything unusual."

"So you don't think there was any foul play?" The taller officer wrote something on a pad.

"No, we don't." Evan pointed where some clothes were. "They took their jackets."

"And a blanket," Julia added as she noticed that one was missing from the foot of the bed.

"But that doesn't mean they can't get them-selves into trouble."

"I agree, Mr. Paterson." The other policeman turned toward the door. "I'll call this in and give them the girls' descriptions and what they're wearing. I'll have the patrols be on the lookout for them."

After his partner left, the other officer said, "It wouldn't hurt to call all their friends and make sure they aren't there. Are there any places they like to go?"

"We've already called their friends. We'll check some of their favorite places." Evan took Julia's hand again and headed toward the hallway.

Outside, after the police left, Evan suggested various areas for their friends to search. "This is my cell number." He recited it and continued, "If you find anything, please call immediately, and I'll let y'all know if Julia and I find the girls."

After Julia finished jotting down everyone's numbers, they all scattered to their respective vehicles. The sound of their engines starting reverberated in the quiet night.

"Where are we going to look?"

Evan strode toward his truck. "The church, since it's closest, then the school."

"How about the park?"

"That, too. It's not far from the church."

Exhausted both physically and mentally, Julia climbed into the pickup. As Evan pulled away from the house, she laid her head on the back of the seat, aching to hold her daughter in her arms.

Please, Lord, keep them safe.

"When we find them, what are we going to do?" Julia peered at Evan's strong profile illuminated by the streetlights. Beneath the facade he projected, vulnerability shone through.

"I don't know." Weariness drenched each of his words.

In the middle of all the feelings swirling around inside her, guilt rose. She should have been watching them closer, somehow prevented this from happening. She knew one thing she would do when she got Ellie back. She would make it clear to her daughter it was over, cut the ties completely with him. She didn't want to be responsible for any more of Evan's pain.

He parked at the church, reached behind the seat for a flashlight and then came around to her side as she descended to the pavement. "We'll look around outside since the church building was locked up fairly early tonight."

"That narrows the search." She was visualizing all the places a small child could hide inside.

"Let's take the playground first. It's lit. I don't see them hiding in places too dark. But then, I didn't see this coming, either."

"I should have. *The Parent Trap* is Ellie's favorite movie." And she'd always wanted a father like so many of her friends had.

"If we could read our children's minds, we could prevent a lot of things from happening. Sadly, we can't." Evan opened the gate to the play area. "I wonder what made them do it tonight. Why would they all of a sudden do something so drastic like run away just to play matchmaker?"

Julia thought about her conversation with Sarah earlier about Evan. Had Ellie or Paige overheard her talking about Evan? Was that what made them do this?

After thoroughly checking out the church grounds, they headed across Veterans Boulevard to the town green where the park was. Once they were under the streetlights, Evan switched off the flashlight.

"I'm considering grounding Paige for the rest of her life." Evan made a beeline for the playground at the other end of the town green.

"I was thinking the same thing. I guess, though, that's probably too harsh."

"Yeah, I guess, but it sure did feel good to say it out loud."

In the distance she saw two small figures on the swing set, pumping their legs to go higher. "That's got to be them." *Please, Lord.*

"They spotted us." Evan hurried his pace toward the two children who were slowing the swings down by dragging their feet on the ground.

By the time they reached Paige and Ellie, the two girls clutched the chains, sitting perfectly still on their plastic seats.

"Are you okay?" Julia asked, nothing else coming to mind as she faced her daughter, who neither frowned nor smiled.

"Yes," Ellie said in a hesitant voice.

"Then will you tell me why you left our apartment without saying anything to me?"

"I told Ellie I could swing higher than her. We decided to come and see who could go the highest." Paige lifted her chin a notch.

Evan stepped forward. "Young lady, do you know how many people are out looking for y'all?"

Eyes round, Paige shook her head.

"Why, Mommy?"

Julia silently counted to ten before answering her daughter. "Because I didn't know where you were."

"We were here." Paige pointed to the grounds.

"Yes and y'all forgot to tell Julia you were going."

"'Cause she wouldn't have let us."

"Exactly, Paige. It's after dark and five-year-olds don't run around town after dark by themselves." Exasperation edged Evan's words to a sharpness.

"I'm six now." Ellie stood.

Julia gritted her teeth. "The same goes for a six-year-old. You both know better."

Evan held out his hand to his daughter who reluctantly rose and grasped his. "I'm too angry to decide what to do about this, except that you're coming home with me tonight."

"I think they should apologize to the people who volunteered to search for them."

"That's a great idea." Evan placed a call on his cell phone, first to the police, then to each group looking for the girls. When he was finished, he said, "Everyone will be back at the apartment in a few minutes."

They quickly made their way to Evan's truck and climbed in. A few minutes later he pulled up to the curb in front of Julia's apartment.

"Paige, you'll tell everyone how sorry you are and then go get your things in Ellie's room. When you get home, you can go right to bed."

"Daddy," his daughter pouted, "we didn't think we were doing anything wrong. We just wanted to go to the park."

"Well, now you know you did." He placed his fist on his hip. "You are never to go anywhere without permission and you know that."

Ellie and Paige trudged up to the porch and plopped down on the top step.

"After they apologize to everyone, I need to have a word with you." Julia waved to Sarah who arrived, followed by Anna and David.

"Knowing how slow Paige gets when she's in trouble, I'm sure it will take her a while to gather her clothes."

When her neighbors appeared, Julia mounted the steps. "Our daughters have something to say to you all. Both Evan and I greatly appreciate your help this evening." She nudged Ellie to stand.

Ellie stared at her feet while Paige looked over the people's heads. "We're sorry," they said in unison.

"Sorry for what?" Sarah, who was in the front of the group, asked. "Ellie, you first, then Paige."

Ellie mumbled something.

Before Julia could say anything about her daughter's apology, Sarah moved forward. "I didn't understand you. Say it again, but this time look at us and say it as if you mean it."

Slowly, Ellie lifted her head. Tears moistened in her eyes. "I'm sorry. I shouldn't have gone to the park."

Paige directed her gaze at her teacher. "I'm sorry, too. We didn't mean for this to happen."

"When we get back from Thanksgiving vacation, we will be having a lesson on safety." Their teacher turned to leave.

Julia's neighbors climbed the steps and went into the house. When the last volunteer disappeared, she said, "Ellie, you need to help Paige get her things together, then you get ready for bed."

Her daughter stuck her lower lip out. "Can't she stay? We promise not to leave without telling you."

Julia shook her head. "People went to a lot of trouble for you two tonight. And frankly, I don't think it was about going to the park to swing." Although she gave the girls time to admit what they had done, they stared at the porch's wooden planks. "Go," she said finally, disappointed in her daughter.

Both girls hurried inside. Julia drew in a deep

breath, gathering strength for what she must do. Having a male friend obviously wasn't an option as long as Ellie saw every man as a potential father.

"I don't think Ellie and I should come to dinner tomorrow."

Evan tensed. "Why?"

I can do this. She flexed her hands then curled them into fists. "Because I—" her lungs seized her next breath for a few seconds "—I love you, and if you can't return those feelings, our relationship will only end up hurting our daughters. It will give them hope where there's none."

Chapter Twelve

Evan's forehead creased. Confusion, surprise and acceptance flickered across his features. "If that's the way you want it."

His cold words drove a spike through her. What had she hoped for? A declaration of love? She knew better than that. *No, I don't want not to see you again, but I don't have a choice.* "It's the way it has to be. I can't have my daughter heartbroken." *Not to mention myself.*

"I understand."

You do? I don't. Why can't you love me? Then we could be a family and make our girls' dream come true.

"I—care about you deeply. You have a right to know that. We could see where it's gonna lead."

"Can you guarantee a future for us?"

He shook his head.

"Then it's best if we cut our losses now. Ellie lost one father. I won't have her lose another. Actually I'm glad this happened tonight. It showed me how desperate our children are."

"You can't live your life totally for your child."

"Yes, I can for the time being. When she's older, she'll understand better." Julia glanced toward the front door to make sure Paige wasn't coming yet. "Besides, you have some issues you need to work out. That became clear to me today." She put her foot on the bottom step. "There's just too much standing in our way. Goodbye, Evan."

Paige trudged down the stairs. Julia rushed up to the porch and crossed to the front door as his daughter pushed it open.

"Good night, Paige." Julia escaped inside before she burst into tears.

She imagined the drill of Evan's gaze on her back and for a moment was tempted to peer back at him. But if she did, she would never be able to walk away from him. Now she had to find a way to avoid him—at least until she could harden her heart toward the man.

The house was too quiet. Evan prowled the rooms, unable to sit still. Stopping at the radio, he flipped it on so that some jazz could fill the silence—anything to stop him thinking about Julia in front of her apartment, hugging herself as if she were cold, telling him they had no future.

The urge to pull her into his arms had overtaken him until he had to clench his hands and stiffen his arms. He'd trembled with the need to hold her, and yet what she had said made sense.

Could he put his past behind him? Could he forgive himself for surviving when so many he'd known hadn't? Could he truly forgive Diane for deserting him and Paige?

Can I ask the Lord for forgiveness?

Because if he couldn't do any of those things then Julia was right—he had no business being with her. She deserved all of him or nothing.

He came back to the kitchen and sat. Planting his elbows on the table, he buried his face in his hands. As much as he hated change, with so much of it in his life lately, he knew he had to make some more on his own or he was going to end up a bitter old man—alone. He rubbed the heel of his palms into his eyes, trying desperately to wash away the picture of that man in his mind.

Lord, I haven't been too attentive in the past few years. I guess it was easier to blame You rather than deal with all my feelings. I can't keep doing that. Paige needs all of me. I turned away from You when I shouldn't have. I doubted You when I shouldn't have. I've been so alone for too long. I need You. Can You forgive me?

Evan dropped his hands away from his face and looked around him, seeing his kitchen with new eyes. He pictured Julia standing at the stove showing him how to cook spaghetti. He saw the two excited girls running through the room and out the back, heading for the barn. The image of Julia and him with their two daughters sitting at the table eating dinner lingered. The laughter they'd shared chased away the loneliness that blanketed him, weighing him down.

How had he managed to mess up the best thing that had come into his life in a long time? He'd pushed Julia away when he should have been pulling her close. He'd used his fear of rejection and the past as an excuse he shouldn't grab what the Lord had given him.

But why shouldn't he? What was holding him back? It certainly wasn't his daughter not liking Julia. She wanted him with Ellie's mother.

Was it Whitney's disappearance? He'd been a soldier himself. He knew the risks, had seen death too many times not to realize that his sister might never come home.

Then it had to be Diane. He hadn't put her walking out behind him as he had thought. He'd finally realized that the moment he had read her journal. The entire time he had blamed her for their failed marriage, but he was equally to blame. He hadn't been able to give Diane what she'd wanted and she'd left him because of that. They might still be together if he had. If the Lord could forgive him for his abandonment, then he could forgive Diane for walking away from their marriage.

He drew in a deep breath, held it for a few seconds, then released it slowly. "Diane, I was wrong, too. I forgive you for leaving, for not talking to me about what was bothering you."

Bowing his head, he stared at the tile floor, the various shades of brown swirling together. Laying his heart bare, he opened himself up to his Father's healing hand.

"Daddy?"

Later—he wasn't sure how long he had been sitting there—he heard his daughter's voice. He looked up, caught sight of the sky becoming lighter beyond the window as dawn approached, then swung his gaze to Paige in the doorway.

He smiled. "You're up early."

"I didn't sleep so good."

"Why not?"

"Are you still mad at me and Ellie?" Her forehead wrinkled into a frown.

On the ride home Paige had told him why they had run away. Julia had been right; both girls had wanted to bring him and Julia together. "No, y'all had good intentions." Then he quickly added, "But that's not to mean I'm not disappointed in your methods."

Paige padded barefooted across the kitchen and embraced him. "I love you, Daddy."

He knelt. "I will always love you to the end of time like the Lord, our Father, loves us when we do things that aren't right."

Her bottom lip quivered. She bit her teeth into it, tears pooling in her eyes. "Me and Ellie just wanted a mommy and daddy."

"I know, princess. But there are some things you need to leave to adults."

"But you like Julia."

"Yes, I do."

"Then why can't Ellie be my sister? I get lonely sometimes. It would be nice to have someone to play with all the time."

"It's more complicated than that." Julia wanted a guarantee, and he knew better than most there were no guarantees in life.

Paige tilted her head to the side. "Why?"

"Well…" He didn't know how to explain to a child how a relationship worked between two people who were married. It was obvious he hadn't gotten it right the first time. Could he a second time? "It just is. You'll understand when you grow up," he finally offered in a weak attempt to say something, hoping she didn't challenge the reply.

"Daddy, that's not an answer."

Caught. He hugged Paige to him and lifted her in his arms. Moving to the chair, he sat and held his daughter in his lap. "Honey, it's not only about my feelings but also about Julia's."

"Oh, I know she likes you. Ellie told me she does. So you don't need to worry about that."

And last night she told me she loved me.

"You said you liked her and she likes you. So what's wrong?"

Good question. What was wrong? Remnants of fear, not easily shed, clung to his heart. "It's not something that can be rushed into."

Her chin came up as she squared her shoulders. "Both me and Ellie can wait until Christmas." She leaned close. "But you might want to seize the moment."

Evan's mouth dropped open, and then he coughed. "Where did you hear that?"

"Miss Olga told me that last week. I asked her why she got red in the face when Reverend Fields came into the room." She grinned. "Daddy, you don't want some other man to catch Julia's eye."

"Did Miss Olga say that, too?"

Paige nodded. "I think she likes the reverend."

His daughter was getting love advice from Olga. Someone definitely needed to fix Anna's mother up with a man. "Yes, I think you're right."

"Call Julia. Invite her again for dinner today."

"She told me she didn't want to come last night, honey."

"Try again. Women change their minds all the time."

"Miss Olga?"

"Nope, Grandma." Paige hopped down and tugged on his arm. "Come on."

His gaze fixed on the phone on the desk in the kitchen. He didn't want to give her a chance to say no, and after last night, he wasn't sure of the reception he'd get.

"She probably needs time."

The look on his daughter's face challenged him. He shifted and started toward the phone. Hand on the receiver, he shook his head.

"No, Paige. This doesn't feel right."

"Daddy!" His daughter put her fist on her waist, much like he did occasionally.

"I think instead of asking her to come to the ranch for dinner, we'll take it to her."

"Surprise her?"

He nodded. "I doubt she has much in the way of food since they were coming out here. Wanna help me cook?"

She brightened with a smile. "Yes!"

Then Evan remembered the still-frozen turkey in the sink. The mounds of ingredients in his refrigerator that Julia had him purchase flashed in his mind. He didn't know what to do with most of them.

"There's just one thing. I need help, princess. I don't know how to cook most of the stuff I have in there." He waved his hand toward the refrigerator.

"Hmm. Too bad Grandma isn't in town." Paige rolled her gaze toward the ceiling, then locked it on him. "How about Miss Olga? I know she would help. Call her."

Should he risk letting one of the most dedicated matchmakers know how he felt? What if Julia sent him away? He would have exposed his true emotions to Olga. His hand wavered above the phone.

Did he have a choice?

Bright sunlight slanted across the living room, in stark contrast to her mood. Julia nursed a cup of coffee, hoping the hot liquid would warm her chilled body. She'd never thought she would be serving pizza for Thanksgiving, but that was about all she had in her refrigerator. She'd planned on going to the grocery store tomorrow.

Maybe she and Ellie would start a new family tradition. Family. It looked like it would be a family of two.

And she would be okay with that, just as soon as her heart stopped aching. It had been for the best that she and Evan parted ways. After Clayton, she knew she needed a total commitment from a man, and Evan wasn't able to give her that.

She and Ellie had made it this long without anyone else. They would be all right.

The ringing of the phone interrupted her reverie. She set her mug on the table and snatched up the receiver with little time to regret answering. She wasn't in the mood to talk to anyone.

"Julia, happy Thanksgiving."

"Mom, I didn't expect to hear from you today."

"Why not? It's Thanksgiving."

"Because you call when Dad isn't there. Dad is there, isn't he?" Even though she was disappointed and upset with her father, she didn't want her parents to argue over her. She'd come to terms with her father's rejection as much as she had with Clayton's.

"Yes, he is. In fact, he's sitting right here next to me."

Julia nearly dropped the phone. "He is?" Picturing her dad's scowl the last time she'd seen him made her tremble. Was he looking at Mom like that right now?

"Yes, and he wants to talk to you."

"No!" She couldn't take his scorn after last night. She felt too raw, vulnerable.

"Julia, what's wrong?"

I failed in another relationship. "I—" She didn't know how to tell her mother, especially because she liked Evan and had approved of him. Although she had thought she'd worked through being rejected, she hadn't realized the residual effect it had on her.

"What's happened? Ellie? Is she all right?"

A frantic ring to her mother's words prompted Julia to say quickly, "Ellie's fine.

She's cleaning her room." The pain in her heart expanded, making breathing difficult.

"I wanted to catch you before you two went over to Evan and Paige's."

"We're not going."

In the silence that followed, Julia's galloping heartbeat roared in her ears.

"Are you two going out for Thanksgiving?"

"No, we're eating here," Julia said as though she wasn't breaking into hundreds of pieces.

"Alone?"

"Yes." Sucking in a deep breath, Julia continued. "Evan and I decided last night not to see each other anymore. It's for the best." *No, it isn't, but I can't force a man to love me, particularly my own father.* The constriction in her throat emphasized her growing anxiety.

"I'm so sorry to hear that, dear."

After another moment of long silence, her mother said, "Your father wants to talk to you."

"He…" Julia couldn't get the next word past the lump in her throat. She didn't want to hear all the reasons she had disappointed him. Those were engraved on her mind forever.

"After talking to you last weekend, I decided something needed to be done about this situation. Your dad and I discussed it—"

"Mom, I can't—"

"Please hear him out. You won't regret it."

"Fine." Desperately, she gathered her protective mantle about her, hoping she wouldn't fall apart. She couldn't for Ellie's sake.

A moment passed, a moment in which she wanted to slam the phone down, a moment in which the past six years flooded her in a deluge of memories.

"Julia?" Her father cleared his throat.

"I'm here." She couldn't think of anything else to say after all these years of not speaking to him.

"I—" He cleared his throat. "I'm sorry. I've…"

Julia's hands shook. Her whole body did. She squeezed her eyes closed, savoring the words she'd wanted to hear for a very long time.

"I've been wrong, as your mother has graciously pointed out to me. She showed me some pictures of Ellie, taken at her birthday party. She's a beautiful little girl. I should never have taken my anger out on her."

"Just on me?"

"I was wrong about that, too." He cleared his throat again. "Your—situation brought back bad memories of my own childhood."

Julia sat up straight. "How?"

"I didn't even tell your mom about this

until Saturday, but my mother wasn't married when she had me. Later, she married Harold who adopted me, but for the first eight years of my life, I..."

The rawness in his voice twisted her gut. She knew that fifty years ago people's reactions were very different when it came to a child being born out of wedlock, much different than they were today. "Dad, you don't have to explain—"

"Yes, I do. Your mother has made it clear to me what I've done. There were children who couldn't play with me because of who I was. I didn't have many friends. I felt like an outcast. I never wanted another child to go through what I did, and yet I treated my own granddaughter exactly like I'd been treated."

Picturing her father, a man who rarely admitted he was wrong, brought tears to Julia's eyes. When he uttered the words, "Please forgive me," tears streaked down her face.

Without any reservations, Julia whispered, "I love you, Dad."

"Julia..." he began in an emotionally-laden voice.

When her father didn't continue, Julia started to say something, but her mother came on the line. "Your dad wanted me to see if it would be all right for us to come at Christmas. He wants to meet his granddaughter."

"Of course it's all right. Is Dad okay?"

"Yes, dear." Her mother lowered her voice. "He's just a little overcome at the moment. Now where's that granddaughter of mine?"

"Mommy, Grandpa was crying when I talked to him. Did I do something wrong?" Ellie snuggled up next to Julia on the couch.

"No, hon. He was happy to finally be talking to you."

"Why haven't I ever spoken to him before?"

Julia tucked Ellie closer. She'd gone over this before with her daughter, but Ellie needed to be reassured she hadn't been the reason her grandfather hadn't been in their lives. "He was very angry with me. I did something wrong, and he was disappointed in me."

"He isn't mad anymore?"

"No, honey. Your grandpa and I had a long conversation before you talked to him."

"He said they were coming at Christmas."

"That's the plan." She kissed the top of her daughter's head. "We'll have to come up with things to do."

Ellie turned her face up toward hers. "We can show them the horses at Paige's. Do you think Grandpa likes horses?"

"I don't know."

"He could go riding with us. Evan says Bessie is *real* gentle."

Other than telling Ellie that they weren't going to eat with Paige and her dad, she hadn't told her anything else. Her daughter had assumed it had to do with what she and Paige had done the night before. She'd been on her best behavior all morning.

"Ellie, about going to the ranch. Evan and I decided last night not to spend so much time together. You and Paige can play together, of course. I know she's a good friend."

Her daughter's smile faded. "She's my bestest friend. We won't ever do that again. I promise, Mommy."

"Honey—" Julia smoothed Ellie's hair away from her face "—it doesn't have anything to do with what you and Paige did last night."

Tears streamed down her daughter's cheeks. She leaped to her feet. "I'm sorry, Mommy. I won't do it again." She whirled around and raced from the room.

Julia sighed. How do you explain to a six-year-old child the intricacies of an adult relationship? *Father, please help me say the right thing. I'm at a loss here. I haven't been very good at relationships.*

Then she thought of the most important relationship—the one she had with the Lord. *His love is steadfast, no matter what. His grace He gives freely. I am perfect in the eyes of the Lord. With Him by my side I can do anything.*

She started for her daughter's bedroom when the chimes echoed through the apartment. Julia halted and turned back into the living room. Crossing to the front door, she checked the peephole. The sight of Evan in the hallway stole her breath. With a trembling hand, she grabbed the knob and pulled.

"Good afternoon. I hope Paige and I aren't too late."

"Late?"

"For Thanksgiving dinner."

"I don't have—I don't understand."

Cradling a paper bag, Evan gestured down the hall where Paige stood next to a large ice chest. The little girl held a second sack. "We have brought dinner to you and Ellie. I didn't want y'all to go hungry."

"You didn't need to worry about that." Julia's heartbeat picked up speed.

"We would like to share Thanksgiving dinner with you, but I'll understand if you just want me to leave the food and go." After placing the sack on top of the cooler, Evan heaved it up against his chest. "We've been cooking all morning."

"I—I..." She was at a loss for words. All she could do was step to the side and allow them into her apartment.

When she closed the front door, he turned to her. "I hope that means we can stay."

The impish look on his face caused her to chuckle. "Since all I have is pizza, yes, you can stay."

"Yea!" Paige shouted as Ellie appeared in the doorway.

"Can we play in my room?" Ellie asked, beaming with a smile.

"Sure. Just no scheming," Julia said in her sternest voice.

"We won't. I promise. We've learned our lesson." Paige put the sack on the ice chest where Evan had placed it on the floor, then hurriedly followed Ellie down the hall.

"Her room is the cleanest I've ever seen it.

When I get home, I should take a picture of it since I'll probably not see it that clean ever again."

"Ellie's is, too. Do you think they have been talking on the phone today?"

"I wouldn't put it past them."

Julia peeked into the two paper bags near the kitchen entrance. "What have you fixed for dinner?"

"Oh, the traditional Thanksgiving dinner with a twist."

"A twist?"

"Yeah, Olga helped me since I didn't have any idea where to even begin. I nearly ruined the turkey and would have if I'd thawed it the way I had started to."

"How?"

"With hot water. Olga straightened me out on that. I gave her my frozen one, and she brought me hers that was ready to go."

"She gave you her turkey? What's she going to fix?"

Evan took the cooler into the kitchen. "She wasn't. Anna had invited her over."

"Then why did she have a turkey?"

He shrugged. "She never said. I'm just grateful she had one since mine was frozen solid."

"So what's the twist?"

He grinned. "We have some Russian dishes, too." He took the sacks into the kitchen and began emptying them.

"Why are you really here, Evan?" She hated to break the upbeat mood, but she couldn't afford to hope and dream.

After all the contents were removed from the paper bags and placed on the counter, he carefully folded them and laid them on top of the refrigerator. "I've done some soul-searching since I left you last night." He opened the ice chest and removed the rest of the dishes. "I hope the meat is still hot. That's why I used the cooler to keep the heat in."

"Evan Paterson, what did you discover?"

He threw her a smile that melted her insides. "That I'm still a lousy cook. Thanks to Olga this meal will be edible."

Marching to where he stood, Julia took his chin and forced him to stop what he was doing and look at her. "No one is going to eat a single bite until you talk to me. Let's back up to that soul-searching you did last night. What conclusions did you reach?"

He grasped her upper arms. "That I love you, and I need to stop running away from that fact."

Her mouth fell open. Evan leaned forward

and gave her a quick kiss on her lips. The pounding of her heart nearly drowned out everything else.

"How did you come to that conclusion?"

"I could say that it was a simple one, but I had to deal with all my issues. And you were right." He leaned back against the counter. "It wasn't my time to die. I can't feel guilty that I lived when others didn't, but I can live my life to the fullest in their honor."

"What about Whitney?"

"With the Lord's help I will deal with it if they discover the body is hers. For a while I'd forgotten how to lean totally on the Lord. I was trying to go it alone." Shaking his head, he gripped the edge of the counter. "I don't want to be alone. I want a complete family."

"And Diane?" Julia held her breath.

"Diane wasn't the only one to blame for the failure of our marriage. I was, too. Her journal helped me to see that, and last night I finally admitted my part in it, too. Once I did, it was easier to forgive her for walking out on me and Paige." His gaze darkened. "I've made mistakes in the past, Julia. I will in the future."

"Do you think you're the only one? I've been

putting myself down because I haven't felt worthy. The problem was I fell in love with you and it scared me."

Evan drew her against him, his arms encircling her. "So what you said last night about loving me wasn't a figment of my imagination?"

"No." She cuddled closer to him. "So, where do we go from here?"

"I want us to date and see where our relationship will lead. We have two little girls to think about. I want us to be sure. When I marry again, it will be forever."

She leaned back and looked up into his handsome face. "I like that plan. Ellie and Paige have had too much turmoil in their lives for us to add any more."

"Speaking of… We should say something to them."

"I'm thinking they know something is up."

He peered over her shoulder. "I wouldn't put it past them to be eavesdropping."

Julia laughed. "Usually I would agree, but Ellie is on her best behavior because of last night."

Cupping her face, Evan brushed his lips across hers. His kiss sent her reeling, and in that moment she knew being with him was where she belonged.

He linked his hand with hers. "Let's go talk to them now."

Julia headed for the hallway with Evan next to her.

In her daughter's bedroom the two girls sat on the floor cross-legged, playing Memory. They glanced up when she and Evan entered.

"We're tied." With Mr. Whiskers sleeping in her lap, Ellie gestured toward her stacked pairs.

"That's a great place to stop for a moment. Evan and I would like to talk to you two."

Paige frowned. "We promise not to leave again without telling you."

He walked to the bed and eased down. "When something is bothering you, I want you to come to me, and we'll talk about it."

Julia settled on the floor next to Ellie. "And that goes for you, too. We've always had an open-door policy in this family. There is nothing you can't tell me. Evan and I know you were trying to get us together like in the movie. Isn't that right?"

Ellie dropped her head and stroked Mr. Whiskers.

Paige nodded. "I told Daddy last night. We want to be a family."

Evan captured Julia's gaze. "Julia and I have

talked. We would like that, too, but it isn't something we can rush into. Y'all will have to give us the time to get to know each other. When we become a family, it will be for all the right reasons."

Julia's heart swelled when she heard the word *when,* not *if.* Hope flared for her future— for Ellie's.

"Are y'all gonna date?" Paige glanced from Evan to Julia.

"That's our plan, but we're also gonna do a lot of things as a family." Evan pushed to his feet. "Finish your game, then wash your hands. Dinner will be in fifteen minutes."

He grasped Julia's hand as he made his way to the doorway.

"We're gonna be sisters. I just know it," Paige whispered loud enough so Julia heard out in the hallway.

"Yeah, I hope they hurry up and decide to marry soon."

"The impatience of youth." Julia shook her head.

Evan chuckled. "It's not only youth who are impatient. But we're going to do this right and be one hundred percent sure or at least as sure as we can be."

As they crossed the living room, Evan's cell phone rang. He dug it out of his jean pocket and answered it.

Julia started for the kitchen to get the food on the table, but when Evan said Mike's name, she halted and waited for him.

"They did? You're positive?" A huge grin spread across Evan's face. "Buddy, that's the best news you could have given me. Happy Thanksgiving."

When he ended the call, he swung Julia around. "He just heard a patrol found Whitney alive." He put her feet back on the floor but cradled her face between his hands. "We have a lot to celebrate this Thanksgiving."

"I love you, Evan Paterson."

"And I love you," he said and sealed his declaration with a kiss.

Epilogue

One year later at Thanksgiving

Julia felt arms entwined around her, pulling her against a solid chest. She nestled into the comforting embrace.

"We have a few minutes alone before the girls and your parents come back from the barn. How about taking a break and paying attention to your husband?"

Julia turned with Evan's arms still around her. "I would, but since you invited everyone under the sun for Thanksgiving dinner, I have a lot more cooking to do. Of course, you could always help me."

The corners of his mouth slashed down in a

mock frown. "And risk ruining the meal. I'd better not."

She playfully hit him on the arm. "I think you only married me for my cooking."

"I'm wounded. I do appreciate your talents— every one of them." He winked. "Are you ready for the big announcement?"

"I wouldn't be surprised if the girls have already told my parents."

"They promised they wouldn't."

"It's hard to keep a secret like that. Why do you think we waited to tell them until this morning that they were going to be big sisters in seven months?"

He pulled her to him. "I guess I can understand. I've had a hard time not shouting it from the rooftop myself."

Dear Reader,

Thanksgiving is one of my favorite times of year. It is a time we give praise to the Lord for His grace and love. It's a time to give praise to Him for sending us Jesus. For Evan, Thanksgiving had become a bad time of year with painful memories of his failed marriage. But Julia changed all that for him, but not before he had to learn to trust again.

I love hearing from readers. You can contact me at P.O. Box 2074, Tulsa, OK 74101, or visit my Web site at www.margaretdaley.com where you can sign up for my quarterly newsletter.

Best wishes,

Margaret Daley

QUESTIONS FOR DISCUSSION

1. Evan thought he had been a good Christian, doing what the Lord wanted. He asked the Lord what he had to do to get his sister back. He didn't understand that sometimes bad things happen to good Christians who have done their best. This made him doubt his faith. Has anything like this happened to you? How did you overcome your doubts?

2. Evan had doubts about his purpose. What is your purpose in life? What are you supposed to do with your life?

3. Evan asked this question: What kind of God would allow a man's legs to get blown off? How would you answer that question if someone said it to you?

4. What is your favorite scene in the book? Why?

5. Julia made a mistake that she was paying for. Guilt plagued her. How do you make amends with yourself over a mistake you've made?

6. Julia's father disowned her for her mistake. Although she acted as if it didn't bother her, it did. Have you ever turned away from someone because of what they did? Did you ever forgive them? How did you feel afterward?

7. Forgiveness is one of my main themes in my books. It is important because we have such little time. Was there ever a time in your life where you found it hard to forgive someone? Did you overcome that? How?

8. Who is your favorite character? Why?

9. Evan could have walked away from his mother-in-law after his wife abandoned him and his daughter, but he thought it was important to have her in Paige's life. So he had to put up with things that he normally wouldn't have. Have you ever had to deal with a person like Evan's mother-in-law? What would you have done in his situation?

10. Evan had seen so much death in his life. He had a hard time dealing with his sister's dis-

appearance in a war zone. What are some good ways to deal with those issues?

11. Being a single parent is difficult. Julia turned to the Lord to help her, while Evan turned away. Evan was trying to do things alone. Julia realized she couldn't, that she needed God. Have you ignored the Lord when you should have been embracing Him? What or who made you change your mind?

12. Both Julia and Evan for different reasons decided that becoming involved in a relationship wasn't for them. When they began falling in love, they panicked. They were afraid of being hurt. Life is a risk and we do get hurt. How do you comfort someone when they are hurt by another?

Love Inspired®
SUSPENSE

RIVETING INSPIRATIONAL ROMANCE

Watch for our new series of
edge-of-your-seat suspense novels.
These contemporary tales
of intrigue and romance
feature Christian characters
facing challenges to their faith...
and their lives!

**NOW AVAILABLE IN REGULAR
AND LARGER-PRINT FORMATS.**

Steeple
Hill®

Visit:
www.steeplehillbooks.com